Until Shiloh Comes

Robert M. Starr

Copyright

This book is a work of fiction. Names, characters, places, and incidents either are products of the author's imagination or are used fictitiously. Any resemblance to actual events or locales or persons living or dead is entirely coincidental.

Copyright © 2009, 2012, 2013 by Robert M. Starr

Scripture quotations taken from the New American Standard Bible®,
Copyright © 1960, 1962, 1963, 1968, 1971, 1972, 1973, 1975, 1977, 1995 by The Lockman Foundation

Used by permission. (www.Lockman.org)

ISBN: 149959853X
ISBN-13: 9781499598537

Dedication

To my beloved wife,

Alyssa

Sometimes, I am not certain whether
she is my strongest supporter
or my toughest critic,
but she keeps me honest.

Other Books by this Author

A Walk in the Wilderness—*Certificate of Merit* winning Christian fiction, 2013 Deep River Books writing contest.

"As I stood up outside the broken airplane, I found that the snowfall of the previous night had ended. The scene before me was bleak, shaded in gray and without the warmth of any color. Even the snow seemed more gray than white, and the trees along the ridges below seemed less green than charcoal. I couldn't see the sky, only the low clouds which held the snow to come. The wind was even stronger than it had been during the night, and I knew there would be no search that day."

Olympic Gold Medalist, World Champion and professional figure skater, Karen Flynn and her younger sister, Amy, crash into the Canadian wilderness on a stormy winter night, with only John Brant, their pilot, to help them. A Vietnam vet and a jungle survival expert, John is out of his element in the frozen wilderness, but he has only himself to rely upon. Karen and Amy need and appreciate his help, but their reliance is on God, a fact John barely tolerates.

Acknowledgments

To **Egon Richard Tausch**, author of *A Voice In Rama: Slaughter of the Innocents*, professor and historian, for his critique and extensive efforts in correcting errors and reconstruction myths in my original manuscript.

"The scepter shall not depart from Judah,
nor the ruler's staff from between his feet,
Until Shiloh Comes,
and to him *shall be* the obedience of the peoples."
Genesis 49:10

CHAPTER ONE

October, 1876

The little girl at the piano was the first to see him ride over the ridge and down into the Montana valley that was her home.

"Rider coming, Mother, leading a packhorse," she said, as she continued to play.

Sarah Hadley walked to the window beside the piano and looked across the wide expanse of grass. The rider was far enough away to be still only a dark silhouette against the pale brown of the autumn grass, but the young woman's breath caught momentarily as she watched him. The rider sat his horse like the cavalry officer her late husband had been. How many times, she wondered, had she watched Jonathan ride across that grass in just such a manner, leading a packmule in from a hunting trip or from a trip to town for supplies?

"Keep practicing, Hannah; he is still a long way off."

Sarah left the window, went out onto the wide porch on the front of the house and stood by one of the massive columns that supported the balcony above. She looked again to measure the rider's progress then turned toward the barn and corrals to look for Caleb Stohr, the one man who had remained on the ranch through the trouble of the past two years. She saw him working his way around the corrals and the creek, approaching the house out of sight of the coming rider. As he reached the side of the house, she moved to the end of the porch to speak to him.

"Caleb, do you suppose he is looking for work?" she asked. "This time of year, he might be looking for a place to spend the winter."

"Could be, Miz Hadley," Caleb agreed. "But he's no broke an' out of work cowpoke, not leadin' a packhorse loaded down with supplies, prospector maybe." He paused a moment, then added. "Ma'am, until we've had a look at him, might be wise not to let on that I'm the only man around the place."

"Caleb, we desperately need help with the work, but I have learned to trust your judgment of men as much as Jonathan did. I know you will not lie to him, and I would not expect you to, but if he is looking for work and you like the looks of him, we should take him on."

"Yes, Ma'am," he said. "I'll wait down by the barn, an' I'll have this old Spencer near to hand."

Caleb left her to retrace his route around the creek and corrals. As Sarah turned back toward the column where she had been watching by the steps, Hannah came out of the house. The little girl stood next to her mother and watched the rider work his horses down the slope toward the beaver pond in front of the house.

"He looks like Father coming home, doesn't he, Mother?" she said.

"Yes, honey, he does. He sits a horse the same way, but that is not your father."

"I know, Mother, but I wonder who he is."

"We shall find out when he gets here. Now go back to your practicing until he does."

During the long ride across the valley, the rider had taken in

8

everything to be seen, the wide, meandering creek, the stand of aspens surrounding the beaver pond, the evergreen forest climbing the mountain foothills beyond the house, bunkhouse and barn. The buildings were well built and in good repair, as were the fences, but it was the house that drew his attention, a large white structure that would have been expected on a southern plantation before the war, but seemed somehow out of place on a cattle ranch many miles from the nearest neighbor. He stopped at the creek before he crossed to let his horses drink, then he rode on to the woman waiting on the porch at the top of the front steps. He was surprised by her youth and beauty. *No more than thirty*, he thought, *probably several years younger.* Her rich, dark hair was shining in the afternoon sun; a look of sadness touched the brilliance of her blue eyes. Her manner reminded him of another young lady standing on a porch just such as this one.

"Howdy, Ma'am," he said, as he removed his dusty wide-brimmed chocolate brown hat. "Ran into a couple of riders a few days back, down on the Powder River, said you might be looking for someone to hire on. Who should I talk to?"

"Caleb is down at the barn," she told him. "You will need to talk to him."

"He your foreman?" the man asked.

"No, sir," she said. "My foreman was killed several months ago."

"Accident?" he asked.

"No, he was murdered, shot in the back. We do not know why, and he was not the first. Does that change your mind about wanting to work here, sir?"

Sarah watched his face for signs of surprise and saw none. His faded blue eyes were steady; the weathered face never changed. He was older than she had expected him to be, some years past forty, but his straw-colored hair had only begun to show white at the temples, and she sensed a solidness about him, a strength of character that was both impressive and somehow disquieting.

"No, ma'am, the riders I met spoke some of the trouble you've had. But I need a place to winter, and it's a little late in the year to be looking for work, so I thought you might be willing to take me on."

"Then ride down to the barn and talk to Caleb," she said.

As he was about to replace his hat, Hannah stepped out onto the porch. She shared some features with her mother, but her hair was blonde, beginning to turn light brown, and her eyes were large pools of dark brown.

"Good afternoon, young lady," he said. "Was that you I heard playing the piano as I was riding across your valley?"

"Yes, sir."

"You play well," he told her. "Much better than I did at your age."

"You play the piano?" Hannah asked.

"I did," he told her. "It's been some time, though. I'm out of practice now."

He replaced his hat and turned his horses toward the barn.

"Mister," Hannah called out. "What's your name?"

He stopped the horses and turned in his saddle to look back at her.

"Folks call me Shiloh."

CHAPTER TWO

Caleb had watched from the shadows inside the barn door facing the house. As Shiloh led his packhorse toward the barn, Caleb leaned his Spencer carbine against the barn wall and stepped out where he could be seen.

"You Caleb?" Shiloh asked, as he looked at the lean old man.

"Yep,"

"Folks call me Shiloh. The lady said I should talk to you about hiring on."

"I 'spect you know somethin' about cattle."

"Worked cattle a few years down in Texas," Shiloh told him. "Then signed on with a trail herd headed for Kansas. Drew my pay there and decided to have a look at the country hereabouts."

"Pay here is forty dollars a month," Caleb offered.

"That's foreman's wages in Texas," Shiloh admitted.

"Miz Hadley tell you we've had trouble on the ranch?"

"She did, but I'd already heard it from a couple of riders I met down on the Powder. Part of the reason I came this way—looking for work this late in the season."

11

"Could get you shot."

"Wouldn't be the first time," Shiloh admitted.

"Might be the last," Caleb added dryly.

"Reckon I'll let God worry about that."

"You a preacher?"

"Nope, just a believer."

"You object to work that cain't be done from the back of a horse?" Caleb asked. "Still got hay an' wood to cut fer the winter."

"I'm willing to do whatever needs to be done."

"Then I reckon you're as big a fool as I am." Caleb grinned. "You're hired."

"Thanks," Shiloh said with a grin of his own. "Appreciate the confidence."

"Let's get yore gear off them horses an' turn 'em out to graze. I usually keep some saddle stock in the barn durin' the night, plenty of empty stalls if you want to bring yores in after supper. We eat at the big house, by the way, an' Miz Hadley is a very good cook—the young'un is gettin' to be"

"Glad to hear it—I've had about enough of my own cooking to do me." Shiloh said, as he eased himself out of the saddle and onto the ground.

"How much of what's on the packhorse will need to go to the bunkhouse?" Caleb asked.

"Not much, most of it's food for the winter, bacon, beans, flour, salt, sugar, coffee, some airtights—peaches, tomatoes and the like. A sack of potatoes, a sack of ear corn and some canned milk. Tools I bought in case I had to build a winter shelter. The tools can be stored here in the barn, reckon the food should go up to the kitchen—no sense in letting it go to waste, and it might save a cold trip or two in bad weather."

"Miz Hadley will prob'ly be willin' to pay you fer it," Caleb told him.

"Well, whatever she thinks is fair." Shiloh said, as he pulled his rifle from its scabbard and stripped the rig off of his saddle horse.

"I'll put yore saddle in the tackroom, while you start on yore packhorse," Caleb offered.

"Thanks."

Shiloh had the tools unloaded from the packsaddle and had stacked a couple of sacks next to his bedroll, saddlebags and rifle when Caleb came out of the tackroom.

"This stuff will go to the bunkhouse," Shiloh said, pointing to the pile surrounding his bedroll. "Any place special I should put the tools."

"That axe an' saw might come in handy at the woodshed, might as well keep everythin' together. Been a long time since I've seen anybody use an adze. You any good with it?"

"I get by when I have to; man that taught me was as good as anyone I've ever seen." Shiloh said. "The rest of what's on the packsaddle should go to the kitchen."

"Why don't I take that up while you get moved into the bunkhouse?" Caleb asked.

"Okay," Shiloh agreed. "Matter which bunk I take?"

"Nope, be just you an' me," Caleb told him. "I have a room to myself, an' there's a room fer the foreman. It's empty now that Jim's dead, might as well move in there fer the winter. Ain't likely Miz Hadley will find anyone else afore spring, prob'ly not until we figure out who's doin' the killin' an' put a stop to it."

"You got any ideas on that?" Shiloh asked.

"Somebody with a good rifle." Caleb said. "Best I can figure, the shot that killed Jim came from seven or eight hunnerd yards off. Not many rifles will reach that far with any accuracy, an' it takes a good marksman behind the rifle."

"Was he robbed?" Shiloh asked.

"Not that a body could tell," Caleb said. "Had a little cash on him—never carried much. His revolver was still in the pommel holster on his saddle. It was roundup; his rifle was in the chuckwagon with everybody else's."

"Killer leave any tracks or sign, casing brass or the like?"

"I found where he shot from, mighty little sign—looked to me like he used a low limb fer a rifle rest. If he did, he's a taller man than me, prob'ly taller than you. An' I think I found where he tied his horse. Not much sign there either, some pressed down grass but no hoof prints. Found a few strands of sheep's wool—made me think he might have wrapped his horse's hooves with sheepskin to hide his tracks. I followed what little trail there was into the rocks then lost it completely."

"Was Jim the third man killed?"

"Unless you count the Colonel," Caleb told him. "Looked like his horse throwed him. That could've been a genuine accident, an' it happened more'n a year before any of the others."

"The Colonel? Who was that?"

"Colonel Hadley, Miz Hadley's husband. He was a Union cavalry officer in the war. Jim an' some of the original hands rode with him back then an' still called him by his military rank, so we all did."

"Anything make you think it wasn't an accident that killed him?" Shiloh asked.

"He was as good a man on a horse as any I've knowed, broke his own string of broncs. Sure, somethin' could've spooked his horse, an' any man can be throwed, but it just didn't *feel* right to me—him landin' headfirst on the only rock around an' bashin' in the back of his head. It'd rained before we got to him—backtrailed his horse when it showed up at the barn without him—so the tracks wasn't clear, but it looked to me like there could've been more'n one horse an' maybe some boot prints—like he stopped to talk to somebody. No other reason I can think of fer him to stop there an' no real reason to get off his horse. If somebody else was there, it had to be somebody he knew an' trusted. The Colonel was still too much a soldier to turn his back on a stranger."

"How were the others killed?"

"Purty much the same as Jim, not from as far away, but far enough to need that same long shootin' rifle an' unusual skill."

"Anything to connect the places where they were killed?"

"Don't think so," Caleb said.

"And nothing stolen?"

"Nope."

"The ranch been missing cattle?"

"Well, we had the worst winter anybody still alive can remember, so we lost some cattle to the cold, but the tally on calves fer them that survived was pretty close. Any stock missin' that weren't killed by the cold could've been got by wolves, maybe an Injun huntin' party or even a cowboy ridin' the grubline."

"Anybody tried to buy the ranch since the Colonel died, or tried to scare folks off before the killing started?"

"Not that's been told to me."

"Well, there has to be a reason," Shiloh said. "If we can figure out why, then maybe we can figure out who."

CHAPTER THREE

Caleb picked up the lead rope and started the packhorse toward the house, while Shiloh gathered up his gear and headed for the bunkhouse. When Caleb reached the back of the house, he tied the packhorse to a hitching ring mounted on a post at the edge of the back porch steps and started up the steps. Before he reached the door to knock, Sarah stepped through the door to meet him.

"What is all this?" she asked, as she looked at the packhorse.

"Winter food supplies Shiloh bought in case he weren't able to find work," Caleb said. "He even had tools to build him a cabin. But he figured we ought to go ahead an' eat the food rather than let any of it go bad. An' I ain't learned to mind my own business. I told him you'd prob'ly be willin' to pay him fer it, since meals are usually a part of his wages."

"So you hired him?" she asked.

"Yes, ma'am," Caleb told her. "I liked him right off."

"Well, I told you to make the decision about him, and you were right that I should pay him for the food," she said. "Will you help me carry it into the root cellar?"

"Yes ma'am."

Sarah was surprised when she found the sacks with potatoes and ears of corn.

"Well, either he is a good cook, or he likes to eat better than the average cowboy."

"Ma'am, he ain't no average cowboy. That there's an uncommon smart man, an', while he didn't say so, I think he come here a purpose, 'cause he knowed you was a woman with a child an' in need of help. I don't know why exactly, but I've got a feelin' about him. He sits a horse like the Colonel did, wears a Colt's revolver an' carries a Winchester rifle like they was a part of him. I'd say he fought in the war, prob'ly cavalry like your husband was an' most likely an officer as well. When I mentioned the trouble we've been havin', he didn't so much as bat an eye, but he knew exactly what questions to ask. An' he's a believer. Yes, ma'am, I think the Good Lord done sent us just the kind of help we need right about now."

"I hope you are right, Caleb," she said. "Let us continue to pray. God knows we need help with the work around here. But I would hate to have another man die trying to help me hold on to the ranch."

Caleb hoisted flour and sugar sacks onto his shoulders then looked back at her.

"When I told him he could get hisself shot just for hirin' on, he said it wouldn't be the first time. When I suggested it could be the last, he just said we ought to let God worry about that. Sounded like good advice to me."

When Caleb had all the food stored in the root cellar or kitchen cupboards, he took Shiloh's packhorse back to the barn, unsaddled him and turned him out to graze. After putting the packsaddle in the tackroom, he picked up his Spencer carbine and headed for the bunkhouse. Shiloh was still arranging his things in what had been the foreman's room, so Caleb stopped and leaned against the frame of the open doorway.

"That the new big-bore 'Centennial' model Winchester?" he asked, waving toward the rifle standing in the corner.

"Yes, I had an 1873 Winchester carbine that I bought down in

Texas along with my Colt's Frontier revolver, both chambered for the 44 Winchester Central Fire cartridge; I carried it until the end of the cattle drive to Dodge City. But I figured the 45-75 cartridge would be a better choice for a rifle in bear country." Shiloh pointed to the Spencer carbine Caleb was carrying. "Picked up a few of those on the battlefields, but cartridges of any kind were hard to come by in the south, so we were mostly limited to what we found with the weapons. Did you fight for the north?"

"Nope, I was too old an' set in my ways to be a part of that foolishness." Caleb ran a bony hand through his thick, white hair. "I come back west with the Colonel's Uncle Ed to stake a claim on this land right after the war started. I'd never been to this country, but Ed had been through here as a young man with Lewis an' Clark an' always wanted to come back here to settle. He was already past eighty when we started west, lived long enough to show me this place an' enjoy a couple of summers. I buried him on the bench behind where the big house is now, stayed on through the war to hold the place fer the Colonel an' his missus." Caleb paused, remembering, a faraway look in his flint gray eyes. "We come west with a pair of Henry rifles an' a good supply of cartridges—good thing we brought a plenty, practic'ly impossible to get 'em out here durin' the war. I'd carried a Hawken fer years an' nearly lost my scalp more'n once trying to recharge that ol' muzzle-loader. The Colonel's cavalry unit used these Spencer carbines through the last years of the war. I liked the Henrys, but they was in purty bad condition from hard use and corrosion by the time the Colonel got out here, so he give me one of the Spencers with loadin' tubes and a Blakeslee cartridge box. With the Spencer, I can still reload in the saddle an' keep shootin', while I'm gallopin' towards anyplace where there ain't no Injuns. Did you run into any Injuns crossin' their huntin' grounds on the way here?"

"No," Shiloh told him. "Might have been different if I had tried to make the whole trip alone. But I left Fort Laramie with a company of cavalry; we joined up with a second company at Fort Fetterman and kept coming north, mostly following the Bozeman Trail into Montana. Eventually, we met a paymaster's wagon and supply train under escort south from Fort Benton. The soldiers I'd traveled with took over escort duties and turned back south with the wagons. I continued north with the soldiers headed back to Fort Benton, stayed with them until we reached the Musselshell, then I followed the river west until I found this ranch."

"I'm surprised them soldiers didn't stir up trouble along the way. Feelin's is runnin' higher'n ever against all the tribes since the fightin' at the Little Bighorn." Caleb observed.

"Some of the men were spoiling for a fight, but a lot of them were raw recruits," Shiloh told him. "The officers went out of their way to avoid trouble. They were surprised we weren't attacked. The captain from Fort Laramie was of the opinion that the tribes had exhausted their supplies of ammunition in the battles that were fought this summer and were unable to press the advantage they'd won."

"Makes sense," Caleb agreed. "The terrible winter took its toll, then Crook's army started the fightin' in spite of the bitter conditions."

"Have the Indians ever attacked this ranch or driven off any of the cattle?" Shiloh asked.

"Nope, maybe 'cause they knew me or knew of me," Caleb said. "I lived among the Cheyenne an' the Sioux at diff'rent times durin' the years I was trappin' beaver. I learned their languages purty well an' can make sign well enough to make myself understood with the other tribes. This ranch was intentionally built west of their favored huntin' grounds, an' the hot springs in the town of Brewer Springs—they're beginnin' to call it White Sulphur Springs now because of the Post Office—are 'wampum waters' for all the tribes; they bring their sick for the healing effects of the mineral water, so they don't make war with each other here. And we prob'ly ain't had trouble 'cause the colonel was

20

willin' to trade an' was generous when the huntin' parties had to come this far lookin' fer game. If we'd seen the buffalo, antelope or elk herds, we'd pass along that information. An' if they rode back empty-handed, the colonel would cut out half a dozen or a dozen young steers for them to drive back to their villages.

"Toward the end of this past winter, twenty Sioux hunters rode up to the house; they was near starved, froze half to death, an' their horses was just as bad off. Most winters, we get some warm spells an' some snow melt, so there's usually some exposed grass fer the stock, an' the wild critters make out purty well. Last winter it never thawed an' the snow was deep. We had to drive our cattle into protected canyons to keep 'em from driftin' to escape the wind. An' we had to feed 'em hay the whole winter—weren't no open grass cured on the stem to graze 'em on.

"Them Sioux had made a wide circle lookin' fer game an' hadn't even been able to feed theirselves. There was no grass fer their horses. They managed to keep 'em alive by diggin' down to expose the grass fer 'em. But that's killin' work fer starvin', freezin' men, an' they couldn't clear enough snow to more than barely keep them animals alive.

"When they showed up here, Miz Hadley had Jim shelter the horses in the barn an' provide hay an' grain fer 'em. Then a steer was butchered and roasted to feed the men. Them braves stayed the night, an' Jim made shore neither our men nor them Injuns was doin' any whiskey drinkin'. Come mornin', Miz Hadley had us round up about fifty head of steers to send back to the villages with the hunters. An' she give 'em enough grain to get their horses home.

"I ain't sayin' we won't never be raided, but Injuns is people; they love their families same as we do, an' they can appreciate kindness same as we can. They do some mighty mean an' hateful things when they make war; so do we. An' some of the things we think are the most terrible, they do 'cause they believe in a diff'rent hereafter than we do. Comes down to ignorance an' our sin natures. Injuns need to come to the Lord same as anybody else, an' it ain't any easier fer them than it is fer anybody else. They're proud; we're proud. An' I don't think the Good Lord has a lot of regard fer proud."

"You certainly can't blame them for fighting to hold on to their way of life. And only a fool would fail to see that we are a genuine threat to them."

"Amen to that," Caleb agreed.

Shiloh pulled the last book out of one of the sacks he'd taken from the packsaddle and placed it on the shelf with several others.

"Always wanted to learn to read," Caleb admitted. "Never found the time and the teacher in the same place."

Shiloh turned from the shelf to look at him.

"Likely to be some time this winter, and I can teach you."

"If we don't get shot first," Caleb said in his wry way.

"Yep," Shiloh agreed. "Been thinking some on that. Did you see the wounds on the three men who were shot?"

"I did, but I reckon I didn't look very close—just to tell they was shot."

"Any of them live long enough to see a doctor?"

"Nope."

"Who prepared the bodies for burial?"

"Miz Hadley done most of what was done."

"She know enough about firearms to make a guess as to caliber or to notice any special characteristics that might help us decide what rifle the bullets were fired from?"

"I doubt it, but it won't hurt none to ask, an' she might still have some of the clothes they was wearin' when they was shot."

"Who investigated the shootings?" Shiloh asked.

"Town marshal took statements from those of us who rode into town to tell him, but his authority only goes to the edge of town. He sent word to the territorial marshal, but that gent ain't got out this way yet."

"I've been trying to think of any rifles with the range and

accuracy to hit a man at the distance you estimated, so far I've only remembered three, the Whitworth, a Remington or a Sharps, but I'd guess there are others, probably some new ones I haven't ever heard of."

"Whitworth, that the English muzzle-loader yore Johnny Reb sharpshooters did so much damage with durin' the war?"

"Yep," Shiloh said. "Killed at least one man from more than a mile away."

"You think some Johnny Reb sharpshooter is still fightin' the war, or out here gettin' revenge against the Colonel's people for somethin' that happened in the war?"

"Maybe, but I doubt it. For one thing, the Colonel wasn't one of those shot. No, I'd guess this has something to do with land or money or both. Anybody struck gold hereabouts? Been a lot of gold strikes in other parts of Montana Territory."

"I done a lot of lookin' fer gold my own self," Caleb admitted. "Never found the first hint of a nugget on this place; ain't heard of nobody finding color close by, an' that ain't an easy kept secret."

"Anything else you can think of that would make somebody want this place?"

"Well, the land an' water, an' the cattle, of course, but there's lots of land an' water free fer the takin', some wild cattle, too, south of here, so I don't know why anybody would go on a killin' spree to get this partic'lar bit of ground. An' it ain't like this is the biggest place around. Of the ranches borderin' us, only the Half Circle C to the southwest is a bit smaller; the Rafter M to the southeast is a good bit bigger. The K Bar T east of us is twice as big, an' the Slash V to the north of us is four times as big. All of 'em has plenty of water. The Colonel laid claim to about three hunnerd sections."

"Got to be something," Shiloh said. "And that's still a big piece of country.

Caleb scratched the white stubble of beard on his chin and rubbed a pattern on the plank floor with his boot toe.

"Some railroad surveyors come through here a few years back; if they planned to run tracks across this place, that might make it worth a whole bunch to somebody."

"It might. Do you know which railroad it was?"

"Nope, I never saw them myself an' never heard anybody say, but we can prob'ly find out next time we're in town. Them boys is bound to have been in the saloon or the general store; same man owns both places. He runs the store an' has some hired help tend bar. We can ask him."

"Probably ought to do it very quietly."

"Prob'ly."

Shiloh pulled his vest off and started unbuttoning his shirt.

"What do you use for a bathtub? Been on the trail for a quite a spell, I'd like to clean up before supper."

"Wash tub's hangin' on the back wall next to the firewood. You'll have haul water from the pump on the well back of the big house, an' you won't get no help with that from me."

"You afraid some might splash on you?" Shiloh teased.

"I got caught out in the rain not more'n two weeks ago, so I don't need no bath!"

CHAPTER FOUR

When Hannah Hadley clanged the triangle to tell them supper was ready, Caleb and Shiloh wasted no time getting to the table.

"Well," Sarah said. "We do not normally dress for dinner, Shiloh, but you look very nice, cleaned and shaved and dressed to dine."

"Thank you, Ma'am," Shiloh said. "Caleb's been bragging on the cooking you two do, and I didn't want trail dust to contaminate good food."

"Thanks to your contributions," Sarah said. "We are having special fare this evening—your corn and potatoes and our beef and beans."

"And a peach pie," Hannah added.

After finishing his first bite, Shiloh stage whispered, "Caleb, did I die and go to heaven?" Before Caleb could answer, Shiloh added, "You did not exaggerate; this is wonderful food."

"I thank you, sir," Sarah said. "But wait until you taste Hannah's pie. You will think this food fit only for animals."

"If that is so, then I shall willingly move into the barn," Shiloh told her.

Sarah noticed that Shiloh's manner and speech had become that of a southern gentleman. She made no mention of the change, but her curiosity about the man increased significantly.

"Shiloh, since moving to the west, and especially since the death of my husband, I have not practiced the kind of entertaining common to the east, but today has become something of a special occasion, and we do have a few bottles of very good wine in the cellar, if you would enjoy a glass with your meal."

"Thank you for the offer, ma'am; there was a time when I would have enjoyed that very much, but I have come to a stage in life where I must refrain."

"May I ask why?"

"For the moment, please simply accept that I can no longer hold my liquor as a gentleman should and allow me to gracefully decline your offer."

"Of course," Sarah said. "I know that Caleb does not care for wine, nor do I truly enjoy it, and I regard Hannah as too young to yet acquire the taste. However, I had planned to offer brandy after dinner, and Caleb does enjoy that. Would you be offended by his having a glass?"

"Not at all," Shiloh told her. "I have no objections to others enjoying themselves. For myself, however, I have found that the only way I can now obey the scriptural teaching to avoid drunkenness is to refrain from any drinking whatsoever."

"I believe, sir, that I understand, and I will endeavor not to become a 'stumbling block' to your continued restraint," Sarah told him then she asked. "Have you long been a believer of the scriptures?"

"Of the scriptures and of God, yes," he told her. "Growing up in the Shenandoah Valley of Virginia, it would have been nearly impossible not to have been, but I have only in recent years come to the knowledge of who Jesus truly is and grown to understand and enjoy true salvation."

"That is another story I would genuinely love to hear, but I sense that it may be related to your need to refrain from strong drink, so I will restrain my curiosity. How ironic that you grew up in the Shenandoah Valley. My husband, Jonathan, served there during the war, finding his duties at the end more distasteful than even the battles he fought in."

And, for Shiloh, the connection was suddenly clear.

"If your Jonathan, Colonel Hadley, was the Colonel 'Black Jack' Hadley who commanded the 10th New York Cavalry, then it is indeed ironic that I should be sitting at this table in this house. He was my adversary from the first day of the war until the last, for I served with the 7th Virginia Cavalry, and while I never met him personally, even after the surrender at Appomattox Court House, our skirmishes were frequent, and I suspect his distasteful duty at the end was following the orders of General Sheridan in burning the farms of the Shenandoah, including my own." Shiloh shook his head sadly at the memory. "If I recall accurately, Sheridan was quoted as saying, 'I want it so barren that a crow, flying down it, would need to pack rations.' I remember the quote, but it may have been General Grant that said it in giving the original order to Sheridan."

"That was indeed my Jonathan," Sarah told him. "He built this house in honor of and as a reminder of those like it that he burned in Virginia. He followed orders, as he felt honor bound to do, and I know that he was deeply injured inside by the battles and the deaths he was responsible for, but he was ashamed only of the destruction of those homes and farms."

"I understand," Shiloh said. "I would have felt as he did and acted as he did. And, as much as it hurts me to admit it, Sheridan's order was a sound military tactic."

"Jonathan agreed," Sarah said. "But it did not eradicate his sense of shame for the actions he took." She looked around the table and realized that all had finished the meal. "Is everyone ready for Hannah's pie? Hannah, would you like to serve?"

"You said you 'served with' the 7th Virginia. Was you an officer?" Caleb asked.

"Yes, at the beginning of the war, I organized and outfitted a cavalry unit of volunteers at my own expense. As a result, I was awarded the rank of Colonel and given command of the unit. We were assigned to Major General J.E.B. Stuart, and I served under him until he was mortally wounded in the battle at Yellow Tavern. Your husband was in that battle as well, Mrs. Hadley. When the General fell, I assumed command temporarily, and though it is most often held to be a confederate loss, we actually turned the tide of battle at the James River and prevented Sheridan from riding straight into Richmond. For my actions, I was promoted to Brigadier General, and my troops thought I should have been given Stuart's cavalry corps command rather than Major General Wade Hampton. But General Lee was faced with the same kind of decision he had to make when Stonewall Jackson was killed. General Stuart was assigned temporary command, led brilliantly, and the troops thought he should have replaced Jackson. But Lee knew that while Stuart had shown himself capable of filling Jackson's boots, he was most valuable and irreplaceable in continuing to provide accurate information in the reports Lee relied on, so Lee gave Jackson's command to Ewell. Perhaps, I could have filled Stuart's saddle, but Hampton was more experienced and proved himself worthy of Lee's confidence almost immediately against Sheridan at Trevilian Station. And like Stuart, Lee already had me serving in the capacity I was most suited for."

"And what was the capacity you were most suited for?" Hannah asked.

"Lightning thrusts and feints, diversions or flanking movements in support of Lee's infantry. Or direct engagement of enemy cavalry, which was often led by your father, Hannah. And in continuing to gather the kind of information Stuart had provided in his reports. Those were the kinds of actions Stuart had trained my unit for, and that's where we were most valuable to Lee."

Shiloh stopped talking long enough to take a bite of Hannah's pie.

"Young lady, this pie is delicious! Will you marry me when I grow up?"

Hannah gave him a scathing look, long accustomed to the teasing of western men, then quipped, "By the time *you* grow up, *I'll* be too old for you."

"Well, then, to ease my broken heart, would you play your favorite piano selection while Caleb enjoys his brandy? Assuming that your mother doesn't mind if I stay up past my bedtime."

"Just a little past your bedtime should be alright; you will enjoy Hannah's playing as much as you have her pie."

Hannah played a beautifully melodious Chopin nocturne. When she had finished, she remained at the piano and enjoyed the applause of the three adults.

"How old are you, Hannah?" Shiloh asked.

"I'm almost eleven."

"How long have you been playing the piano?"

"I started learning when I was five."

"And who is your teacher?" he asked.

"Mrs. Reardon, our pastor's wife."

"How often do you have a lesson?"

"From spring through the fall, usually once a week on Saturday afternoon. We go to town, I have a lesson; we spend the night in town, attend church on Sunday morning and come home in the afternoon. During the winter, we miss church, and I don't get a lesson when the weather is bad."

"Mrs. Reardon has taught you very well," he told her. "Your posture is perfect, your fingering technique is excellent, and your phrasing is exceptional for one so young."

"What do you mean by 'phrasing'?" Hannah asked.

"Obviously, she didn't have to teach you that, you must do it naturally," he said. "Phrasing is the way you group the notes together. In language, you arrange words into sentences, and longer sentences can be broken into phrases. If you listen to a beginner read aloud, you may have trouble understanding, because he will be concentrating on sounding out the individual words and not the ideas and meanings contained in the phrases, but as his reading improves you will be able to understand him clearly, because he will no longer struggle with the individual words, and his eyes will naturally pick up the complete phrases and sentences, so that he can convey meanings rather than just sounds.

"A well-written poem, when read aloud, uses phrasing to convey rhythm and meter, meaning and emotion. Music uses phrasing to convey melody and harmony and so many shadings of sound and emotion. And beginning musicians, like beginning readers, often concentrate so hard on the individual notes that they lose the flow of the musical phrasing. But you are skilled enough at reading music that individual notes no longer trouble you, and you have already, and apparently quite naturally, mastered the technique of musical phrasing. You are very gifted."

"Ann, Mrs. Reardon, says that Hannah is the most gifted student she has ever taught," Sarah said.

"I can easily believe that," Shiloh said. "I don't believe I've ever taught a more gifted student." He looked at Hannah. "I noticed one small thing, a quite common problem that is troubling you. May I help you with it?"

"Yes, I would appreciate any help," Hannah said.

"Do you have the sheet music for the piece you played?"

Hannah pulled the music from a stack of pieces she was learning to play. Shiloh opened it and put it in place in front of her.

"Begin here and play to here," he said and pointed to the sheet music to indicate the section he meant. When she had played it, he pointed to the music again and asked, "What happens when you get to this chord?"

"I can't quite reach all of the notes," she said. "My hand is too small."

"But you try anyway, and end up hitting a note that doesn't belong?"

"Yes."

"And that frustrates you very much, doesn't it?"

"Yes, it does."

He took her left hand and placed it in his right.

"Your hands will probably grow a bit more, but they will never be as large as mine. That is quite natural. For the chord in this piece, you can play the written notes by using your left hand for three of the notes and your right thumb for the fourth note in the chord. That means you will also have to change the fingering for the right hand and play the melody note with your little finger at the same time." He played it for her. "You can learn to do it that way with practice, and it works for this piece. But many times, perhaps most times, your hands will be too far apart on the keyboard, or both hands will be too busy for one to share the work of the other. So then what choice do you have?"

"To leave out one of the end notes in the chord?" she asked.

"Very good, Hannah, that is exactly what you can do. And most of the time, no one will be able to tell that you haven't played every note. You just choose not to play the note that is least noticeable when left out. Can you guess what the third alternative is?"

"Could I play a slightly different chord, one I could easily reach?

"Yes," he agreed. "A chord that still harmonizes or blends with the melody of the note or notes played by the other hand. And if you find that it still frustrates you when you can't play the notes exactly as they are written, I want you to remember this: The Bible says we are 'fearfully and wonderfully made.' There may always be chords that you can't physically play, but you can still play the music beautifully. And God created each one of us to be perfectly suited for His plan. When you find His purpose for your life, you will find that you are perfectly created to accomplish that purpose with His help."

"Have you found God's purpose for your life?" Hannah asked.

"No, Hannah, I haven't; I've only recently started looking for that purpose. But I know a man who has found his purpose, the man who first told me what I've just told you, and even I can see that he is perfectly suited to that purpose. The man isn't perfect, but he is perfectly suited to do God's work. I believe the same thing will be true for both of us."

"I hope so," Hannah told him.

Sarah, somewhat reluctantly, interrupted them.

"Hannah, I have allowed you to stay up quite a little while past your bedtime, but you need your rest, so please tell the gentlemen good evening then go up to your room and get ready for bed. I shall come up in a few minutes to say our goodnights and turn out your lamp."

"Yes, Mother." Hannah hugged Caleb, as was her lifelong habit, hesitated a moment then impulsively and somewhat awkwardly hugged Shiloh before going to her room.

"Since her father died, music has been her one source of joy," Sarah told Shiloh. "Thank you for taking the time to help her."

"She has a rare musical gift, so what I did was of little significance," Shiloh said. "More importantly, she is a very sweet young lady, and that is very much a result of the time you have taken in teaching her."

"Perhaps, but I think it is her nature more than my teaching."

"Her good nature is the Lord's gift," Caleb said. "But Shiloh's right; you're doin' a good job of trainin' her up in the way she should go."

"Thank you, Caleb; I am glad that you think so."

"I do," he said and tried to stifle a yawn. "Reckon it's past my bedtime, too, so I'll be headin' fer the bunkhouse. See you in the mornin', Miz Hadley."

Taking the hint from Caleb, Shiloh retrieved his hat from the hat tree and started to follow, then paused in front of Sarah.

"Caleb told me you made most of the burial preparations for the men who were shot, so I need to ask a few unpleasant questions about them. I didn't think it appropriate to ask in front of Hannah. Can you take a minute before you go in to her?

"Of course," she said.

"Do you still have any of the clothing the men were wearing, a shirt or something with a bullet hole in it?"

"No," she said. "Most of their clothes were badly stained and had absorbed the odors of death. I tried at first to clean some of them then I just burned them all."

"Do you have any experience with bullet calibers?" he asked. "Would you have any idea what caliber rifle might have been used?

"I am afraid not," she said. "I had never before dealt with someone who had been shot. I have never even had to deal with an animal that has been shot. Caleb butchers the meat for me now, but I have always had someone to save me the unpleasantness—my father or my husband. I did what I felt I needed to do for the men who were killed, but I would not know one caliber from another." She held up a slender index finger. "I would guess the holes were about this size, and I did find one thing curious—I expected the holes to be round, but none of them were—they looked like they had been made by a tiny hex-shaped cookie cutter."

"Thank you very much, ma'am. I'm sorry I had to remind you of such unpleasantness, but you've told me exactly what I needed to know." Shiloh looked at Caleb. "It was a Whitworth rifle, and the south didn't get a great many of those through the northern blockade." He turned back to Sarah. "Good night, ma'am. Thank you for a delicious meal and a very pleasant evening. When you say goodnight to Hannah, thank her again for entertaining us and tell her the music she chose as her favorite is also a favorite of mine."

"I shall," she said. "And a good night to both of you."

"Just because it's a Whitworth rifle that still don't necessarily mean the shooter is a southerner," Caleb said, as they walked toward the bunkhouse.

"No, it doesn't," Shiloh agreed. "Most of the southern soldiers had to turn in their weapons at the end of the war. And a northern soldier might have picked up one of the Whitworth rifles on the battlefield. But it doesn't have to have been from the war. That rifle earned a well-deserved reputation. Anybody might have ordered one from England after the war."

"Might be able to track the rifle through the bullets. What is it they call 'em—bolts?"

"Yes, but the rifles come with a bullet mold, to make either the hex-shaped bolts or cylindrical ones, so a man would only have to buy lead to make them, not the bolts themselves. Most of the sharpshooters in our units had the cylindrical molds, kind of surprised me to learn that when fired the pressure would mold the bullet into the shape of the barrel, so even the cylindrical bolts made hex-shaped holes when they reached a target."

The two of them stopped at the barn to let a couple of saddle horses into stalls.

"Caleb," Shiloh said. "I don't know what you've got planned for tomorrow in the way of work, but I'd like to spend some time getting the lay of the land. And over the next several days, maybe you can show me where the shootings took place. Might start with the place the rifleman was hiding when he shot Jim."

"Okay, an' it'd prob'ly help fer you to get a look at the map the Colonel an' his soldiers made of the place."

When they reached the bunkhouse, Shiloh stopped at the door to his room.

"Good night."

"See you at breakfast," Caleb said.

"What time?" Shiloh asked.

"Usually about first light, Hannah likes to clang that triangle about as much as she likes playin' the piano, so you'll likely hear it." Caleb told him. "An' I usually wake up as hungry as a bear that's been hibernatin' all winter, so the music from that triangle is just as purty to me."

"I'll likely wake up on my own," Shiloh said. "But if you don't see me up, would you mind seein' that I'm awake?"

"I might even haul water from the pump fer that."
"And I might have to warm things up with some hot lead!"
Caleb grinned at him and turned toward his bed.
"See you at breakfast."

CHAPTER FIVE

After breakfast, Sarah led Shiloh and Caleb into the room that had been the Colonel's study so that Shiloh could look at the large map that hung in a frame on the wall.

"Make yourselves at home, gentlemen," Sarah said. "I need to go help Hannah clean up the breakfast dishes.

As she left the room, the men turned their attention to the map.

"Jim was workin' back in this canyon when he was shot," Caleb said and pointed a bony finger to the northern edge of the map. "He was 'bout a mile from the line cabin where we was brandin' that day, here, an' from the tracks on the ground I'd guess he'd gathered fifteen or twenty head an' was pushin' 'em along Willow Creek toward the cabin. He was shot from right here." Caleb pointed at a ridge marked on the map. "From out here at the end of this ridge, the killer could see most of the canyon, an' Jim had to ride past him to get out. Best I can figure, Jim was lettin' his horse drink from the creek when he was shot."

"Who all knew where Jim was going to be working that day?" Shiloh asked.

"Anybody workin' the roundup knew. Jim gave the assignments at breakfast that mornin' an' told everybody where he would be."

37

"Who all was at that roundup?"

"Well, besides our hands, there was at least one rep from the dozen or so ranches around, an' there was full crews from the closest ranches. Prob'ly forty or fifty men."

"I see brands for ranches on three sides," Shiloh said. "What's to the west?"

"Some purty big mountains, the Big Belt range."

"Any kind of an easy pass through those mountains, one that a railroad might use?"

"Maybe over a ridge an' down Deep Creek to the Missouri River," Caleb said. "But the easiest way would be to go north or south an' around the mountains. Kinda depends where they'd be wantin' to go with their railroad."

"Tell me about the other two men who were shot."

"Both of 'em served in the war with the Colonel, just like Jim," Caleb said. "Jim was his captain, Tom was a lieutenant an' Red was a sergeant. All three were loyal men an' would have stood by Miz Hadley in any kind of trouble, figured that's what got 'em killed."

"Where were they when they were shot?"

"Tom was the first, about this time last year. He'd been to White Sulphur Springs to mail some letters for Miz Hadley an' was bringin' a few supplies back on one of the packmules. He'd stopped by a line cabin on the Slash V, had some coffee an' grub with a couple of hands there, nothin' unusual in that, we've had good neighbors hereabouts, try to be good neighbors, so any rider is welcome at any cabin or camp come chow time. Them two Slash V hands was the last to see Tom alive, 'cept fer the killer. When he didn't make it back that night, Jim sent three of us to look fer him the next mornin', a youngster named Jack—I didn't much cotton to him an' was glad when he drew his time an' rode off—Red an' me. We come upon Tom's horse a mile or so from the ranch house, dried blood on his neck an' in his mane, the lead rope of the packmule still tied to the saddle, the two of them headed fer the barn. Found Tom a couple of hours later, on the crest of a long rise where he prob'ly stopped to give the animals a blow. Didn't find exactly where he was shot from, but I figured it was from a bench along here." Again, he pointed to the northern edge of the map, this time a little closer to the center. "From where we found Tom, the killer had to be at least three hunnerd yards off, maybe as much as five."

"And nothing was missing?" Shiloh asked.

"Well, it didn't look like it. Everythin' he'd been told to buy was on the packmule, don't know that anythin' was missin' from his saddlebags. He'd bought hisself a drink at the saloon an' some hard candy at the general store, had a few coins in his pocket."

"Do you know if he talked to anyone in town, a stranger or maybe a rider in from one of the other ranches?"

"Nope," Caleb said. "But it's possible. Bartender said it was slow that time of the mornin', didn't remember anybody else in the place at the time. Now that I think on it, I do recall that the storekeeper did say Tom spoke to a lady an' her daughter, just friendly like, in passin', but it didn't seem that Tom had had trouble with anybody."

"What about Red?"

"He an' the youngster, Jack, had spent most of the winter at the line cabin where we was brandin' when Jim was shot. It was early spring, durin' the night somethin' had spooked their horses. Jack said Red figured it was a cougar he'd seen a couple of days before. One of the horses kicked down a section of fence an' the whole bunch took off. At daybreak, Red sent Jack out on foot to look fer the horses while he stayed to fix the corral fence. Jack was maybe half a mile from the cabin an' had spotted several of the horses when he heard the shot. It took him a half hour or so to catch him a horse an' ride back. Red was shot from the trees about four hunnerd yards in front of the cabin."

"You think it might have been the killer who spooked the horses?" Shiloh asked.

"I figure so," Caleb agreed. "And if he knew anythin' about the two men, he would've knowed Red would send the youngster after the horses."

"Why's that?"

"Red limped some from a sword wound he got durin' the war, pained him to walk."

"What about the Colonel?" Shiloh asked. "Where was he?"

"It was the middle of the June just over two years ago," Caleb said. "The Colonel rode over to the Half Circle C to talk to Charlie Carter about the 4th of July party the Colonel held every year. I don't know what they talked about exactly, but as far as I know, it was friendly."

"And the Colonel was thrown from his horse on his way back from the Half Circle C?"

"Yep."

"When did all of the old hands leave?" Shiloh asked.

"Well, the Colonel brought a dozen men with him drivin' freight wagons shipped to the railhead. The first summer they put up the house, bunkhouse and barn. Ed an' me had built a small cabin, but it's gone now. The followin' spring they rode down to Kansas, bought a cattle herd an' drove 'em up here. Lost two men on that drive, one crossin' a river, one in a stampede; they was buried on the trail. Two left to look fer gold. Lost a man from time to time over the years to accidents; eight are buried next to the Colonel an' his Uncle Ed up on that bench behind the house. Jim was the last, an' I had to shame the new hands we'd hired over the years just to get 'em to finish the brandin' an' drive two hunnerd head of yearlin' steers north to Fort Benton. Then they lit a shuck, all six of 'em."

"The goldseekers leave before or after the shooting started?"

"Before," Caleb told him. "They left before the Colonel died."

"So the three that were shot were the last of the original crew—except for you?"

"Yep."

"Well, that tells me something," Shiloh said. "I just wish I knew what."

Shiloh studied the map carefully for a few minutes, asking Caleb an occasional question about trails, grass, watering holes and habits of the herd. Then the two men went out through the kitchen, saying goodbyes to Sarah and Hannah, climbed aboard the horses they had saddled and ridden up before breakfast then rode northwest toward the canyon where Jim was killed. As they left the house, Shiloh looked up toward the bench then turned back to look at Caleb.

"What's back up in those trees?" he asked. "Any kind of cave or natural shelter in the rocks?"

Caleb thought about it for a minute or so.

"There's a rock face that's crumbled an' fallen away, left an undercut with an overhang—might use some of the rocks to wall in that undercut."

"Any caves anywhere else on the ranch?"

"A couple that I know of; one's a couple of miles off an' pretty good sized from what I was told. Likely used by hibernatin' bears."

"The Colonel ever give thought to storing a few supplies inside and using it as a place to retreat to in case the ranch house was attacked and overrun?"

"Not that I know of," Caleb said; he hesitated a moment, then added. "But he dug a tunnel from the root cellar under the house all the way back into the trees."

"Any place back there to pen a few horses out of sight?"

"No, but it wouldn't take much work to make a place."

"Might be a good idea to keep some saddled horses up there, looked like you've got plenty of extra saddles in the tack room. We could take four up every morning before daylight, so a watcher wouldn't be likely to see us, then change those out with fresh horses after dark."

"Prob'ly need to keep some hay an' grain up there," Caleb

added. "But it sounds like a plumb good idee to me."

"That cave you told me about anywhere near the trail we're taking today?"

"Nope, it's off to the northeast."

"Can you get to it from behind the house with pretty good cover?"

"Prob'ly stay in the trees the whole way."

"Maybe we ought to ride that way tomorrow."

"Remind me to bring a lantern from the bunkhouse," Caleb said. "An' you be sure to bring that big-bore Winchester an' plenty of cartridges, just in case that cave has already been laid claim to by an ornery grizzly."

"Might be a sweet, cuddly she-bear; just imagine how warm you'd be snuggled up next to her on a cold winter's night."

"Reckon that'd be just fine 'til she woke up an' figured on me bein' her next meal."

"Tough and stringy as you are," Shiloh said. "She probably wouldn't take more than a bite or two—likely she'd spit out the first bite."

"Are all Johnny Rebs as full of the milk of human kindness as you?" Caleb asked.

"From the day we're born."

"I reckon some of that milk had done soured before it was fed to you."

The two men rode on for several hours with Caleb pointing out features and landmarks or answering questions from Shiloh. They spent another examining the ground where Jim was killed and the spot where the killer had fired from.

"The man we're looking for is more than just a skilled sharpshooter," Shiloh said. "He's an experienced manhunter. And he knows his way around in rough country. You're likely right, unless he had something to sit on, he'd have to be taller than either of us to use the limb he did for a rifle rest. That'd make him a head taller than the average crowd."

"You think it likely he had somethin' to sit on?" Caleb asked.

"Well, probably not something he brought for that purpose—he wouldn't have known where Jim was going to be early enough, and anything out of the ordinary was sure to be remembered, but he could have used his saddle or a rolled up winter coat."

"Which means we still don't know much that's goin' to help us find him."

"Let's ride on over to the line cabin," Shiloh said. "We can make some hot coffee to go with the lunches Hannah packed for us then we can take another look at those woods in front of the cabin."

They were less than a mile from the line cabin, so the ride took less than a quarter hour. With tin cups filled with hot coffee, the two men sat on the ground and leaned back against the repaired corral fence.

"The killer had the sun behind him," Caleb commented. "Red would have been lookin' purty much directly into it—not likely he would have been able to see anythin' even if he was lookin'."

"And there would have been no glare from the lens on a telescopic sight or from field glasses," Shiloh added. "More proof that our killer knows what he's about. You didn't find the place he shot from here or where Tom was shot. Could the killer have been rushed or gotten careless when he shot Jim?"

"Maybe," Caleb said. "But maybe I missed somethin'; I had more ground to cover an' took less time in lookin'."

"Did you look for tracks behind the cabin that he might have left if it was him that spooked the horses?"

"I looked," Caleb said. "Didn't find anythin' I could be sure wasn't left by Jack or Red."

When they had finished their meal, they rode over to the woods across from the cabin and walked the ground just inside the trees.

"I figured about here was the best place to shoot from, but I didn't find anythin' on the ground."

"Did you look up there?" Shiloh asked as he pointed into the huge spruce they were standing next to, a tree that had been large when the surrounding trees had first pushed through the earth. "Our sharpshooters liked to shoot from trees during the war."

"Reckon I ain't thought about climbin' trees since I was a boy," Caleb said. "That never once occurred to me."

Shiloh stripped off his heavy coat and his pistol belt.

"I'll go up and have a look."

Shiloh pushed his way into the heavy lower branches and began climbing close in to the trunk. About ten feet up, he found a scuffed place in the bark that might have been made by the sole of a boot; at twenty-five feet he found what he was looking for.

"I found his nest," Shiloh called down. "If the wind was as still as it usually is at first light, he had a perfect perch. Looks like he had to crawl out to trim a few small branches to make a hole to shoot through, and . . ." Shiloh stretched out on the limb toward the hole in the foliage. "Our sharpshooter must have hurried for some reason, or been careless for the first time; he left something behind."

Shiloh climbed down and handed Caleb a small piece of green cloth.

"What do you make of that?"

"Well, it ain't homespun, good cloth, could be from a shirt or britches, the color of green is about the same as the needles on the tree. But it appears to mean somethin' special to you."

"Berdan's yankee sharpshooters wore green uniform shirts so they would blend into the woods better, and they also liked to shoot from trees."

"So now we have a killer wearin' a yankee uniform an' shootin' a Johnny Reb rifle?"

"Looks like it," Shiloh agreed.

"Would've been easier if he was British," Caleb said. "You can see one of them redcoats from a long ways off. Didn't Berdan's outfit use a special model of Sharps rifle that was named after him?"

"They did, accurate out to eight hundred or a thousand yards."

"Then why would our killer trade his Sharps fer a Whitworth, if he was one of Berdan's outfit?"

"Well, the Whitworth will shoot about twice as far, but we could be hunting a hired killer who's done some studying and uses every trick he's ever learned.

"Could be," Caleb agreed. "He's good enough in the woods to out Injun an Injun; he ain't left us much to find. He's fired three rounds from farther than most folks can see, an' he ain't missed yet."

CHAPTER SIX

Instead of riding out to look at the cave, the next morning Shiloh and Caleb hitched a team to the carriage and, shortly after breakfast, Shiloh helped Sarah and Hannah aboard for the long drive into White Sulphur Springs, while Caleb put their bags in the boot.

"While you're gone, I'll have a look up there on the bench fer a place to pen some saddle horses," Caleb told him. "It's a long drive to town; you keep a close watch on yore backtrail."

"You do the same," Shiloh said.

The long drive to town seemed shorter as the three told stories of favorite moments in their lives. Hannah told Shiloh of a hidden meadow she had found on the ranch, her "favorite place on earth," and made him promise to go with her to see it. Sarah told stories of her youthful adventures in upstate New York, many of which Hannah had never heard. And Shiloh dredged up stories, every pleasant one he could remember, of his boyhood on the Virginia plantation, most of them involving a hound dog named Blue and a bay gelding called Sir Galahad. Each story one told seemed to stir the memory of another, so that they were still in animated conversation when Shiloh brought the team to a halt in front of the hotel.

"I shall arrange for a room for you, Shiloh," Sarah said, as he helped them onto the boardwalk and lifted their luggage out of the boot.

"No need, ma'am," he said. "The livery stable hayloft will suit me fine."

"I am quite certain that you have slept in worse accommodations during the course of war and driving cattle, but there is no need to sacrifice your comfort on this trip. Besides," she said with a wide grin that only partially concealed her seriousness. "Should we ladies become two damsels in distress during the long night, the livery stable is too far away for a knight in shining armor to come quickly to our rescue."

Shiloh swept off his hat and bowed with a flourish.

"Your wish is my command, fair lady!"

Hannah burst into delighted giggles.

"Shiloh, once I've had a chance to freshen up," she said when she had managed to stop giggling. "Would you drive me to the church for my music lesson?"

"Of course," he said. "How much time do you need?"

"Half an hour," she said.

Shiloh made a big show of pulling his watch from his vest pocket to check the time.

"I shall call for m'lady at precisely twelve noon."

"At which time," Sarah interjected. "We shall all dine here at the hotel, before you go off to your piano lesson."

"Isn't Mother always the practical one?" Hannah asked.

"It would appear so," Shiloh agreed. "My starving stomach applauds her."

After the extra room had been arranged for with the hotel clerk, Shiloh carried their bags upstairs then left the ladies and returned to the street, stopping at the carriage long enough to remove his duster, beat some of the dust from his hat and lead the team to the watering trough in the center of the street. After returning the carriage to the hotel and tying the team to the hitching rail, he crossed the street to the general store. He was not in need of anything in particular, other than information, so he browsed through a catalog as he waited for the storekeeper to finish with a customer.

"You got any 45-75 Winchester Central Fire cartridges?" he asked.

"Should have a few boxes still," the storekeeper told him. "Starting to sell a fair number of them and the 45-60 rounds, enough that I ordered a couple of the new big-bore rifles—thought they ought to sell good in bear country."

"That's why I bought mine," Shiloh told him and decided to buy the ammunition. "I'll take whatever you have in stock."

As the storekeeper was pulling three boxes off the shelf, Shiloh kept him engaged in conversation.

"A trail rider told me some railroad surveyors were through here a while back; thought I might try to get work if they're going to start laying track. You heard anything about that?"

"I remember a group came through here, but that was several years back, haven't heard anything since."

"You happen to remember which railroad they worked for?"

"Northern Pacific," he said.

"Thanks," Shiloh said as he paid for the cartridges. He turned away from the counter then turned back as if he had just remembered something else. "You ever get any call for Whitworth patent bullets?"

"Funny you should ask," he said. "I've only seen one Whitworth rifle in my life, fellow came through with one a few years after the war, prospecting, he was. He ordered a hundred of the bullets; never came back for them—heard he was bushwhacked for a bag of gold nuggets. The bullets sat on my shelf for years, in the way, just something else for me to dust. Fellow came through last week and bought 'em all. Said he didn't have a rifle, said they was becoming collector's items back east. Tall, thin man, wore a black frock coat and a planter's hat."

"Doesn't sound like anyone I know," Shiloh said. "Knew a fellow who carried a Whitworth during the war, short, wiry man, rifle was longer than he was tall. Heard he might of drifted this way."

"Wasn't the prospector; he was short, but he was stout."

"Oh, well, if the fellow I'm looking for is in this country, our trails are bound to cross one of these days."

"More'n likely," the storekeeper agreed. "For such a big country, news covers it like wildfire."

"Thanks again," Shiloh said and headed for the door.

"Thanks for the business," the storekeeper said.

As Shiloh stepped out onto the boardwalk, a slightly shorter, but massively built, redhead separated himself from a group of cowhands and approached him.

"Not much good at remembering names," he said with a thick Irish brogue, cautious that a man he knew well might have come west with a new name. "But I rarely forget a face, and I believe our trails have run together in years past." He stuck out his hand. "Michael O'Brien."

"Shiloh."

After a firm handshake, the Irishman tilted his head toward the saloon next door and winked a pale blue eye.

"Buy you a drink?"

"I've had to give up Irish whiskey," Shiloh told him. "But let me buy you one."

"Ah, lad, after all these years, still a man after me own heart!"

At the bar, Shiloh ordered a whiskey for the Irishman and a beer mug full of water for himself.

"Make that two whiskeys, Smoke," O'Brien said with a big grin. "I hate to drink alone, laddie, so I'll just be havin' a second one for you."

"You big mick, you haven't changed a bit."

They found a relatively quiet corner table in the already crowded saloon and sat down across from one another.

"Sergeant Michael Patrick O'Brien, wandering warrior, fighter for lost causes—been a lot of years old friend."

"It has indeed, General, sir," O'Brien agreed. "What's with the name? We weren't anywhere near that battle. You get your name on a wanted poster somewhere?"

"Not that I know of," Shiloh told him. "Just needed something more anonymous when I got off a ship in Galveston, Texas, a few years back. That was the first name that popped into my head— something from the Bible."

"What are you doing in Montana?"

"Started riding for the Hadley ranch a few days ago," Shiloh told him.

"The J H Connected," O'Brien said, calling the ranch by its brand. "Talk about a fighter for lost causes, you know someone is shooting folks out there?"

Shiloh nodded.

"I'm riding for the Slash V," O'Brien told him. "I could draw my time and ride that way looking for work."

"We could sure use you," Shiloh said. "But hold off a while. I'm not sure who we're up against; you might be able to help more from the outside. The killer is shooting a Whitworth rifle, maybe wearing a green uniform shirt from Berdan's yankee sharpshooters when he goes hunting folks. Could be a tall, thin man seen wearing a black frock coat and a planter's hat, bought a hundred Whitworth patent bullets in the general store last week."

"Doesn't sound like anyone I recognize," O'Brien said. "But I'll keep my eyes and ears open."

Shiloh checked the time on his pocket watch.

"Listen, Michael, I have to meet the boss lady and her daughter for dinner, but we need to talk someplace quiet. Any chance you could meet me somewhere out on the range in two or three days?"

"You know where the north line cabin is on the J H Connected?" O'Brien asked.

"One of the few places I do know; I was out there yesterday."

51

"Well, the Slash V has a line cabin about five miles northeast on the North Fork of the Smith River. I'm supposed to ride out there with supplies on Wednesday. If you follow Willow Creek north a couple of miles from your line cabin, you'll see a rock outcropping on the east side with a big lightning-struck tree standing all by itself on top. There's a small canyon with a seep of water and a fire ring just southeast of that outcropping. I can meet you there an hour or so after noon."

"I'll have coffee on."

"Well," O'Brien grinned again. "I guess I can drink that if there's no Irish whiskey."

They shook hands again. Then Shiloh grabbed up his cartridges and crossed the street to the hotel. He took the stairs two at a time, dropped his cartridges in his room, and knocked on the door of the Hadleys' room just as his watch ticked noon. Hannah opened the door instantly.

"Exactly on time," she said with a grin.

Shiloh escorted the Hadleys downstairs to the dining room. As he was seating them, a tall, handsome man in his thirties walked up to their table. His medium brown hair was slightly mussed where he had removed his hat, but his clothes were perfectly tailored to his muscular frame. His cold, brown eyes looked hard at Shiloh, then they softened into slyness as he turned toward Sarah.

"Hello, Sarah, you look lovely, as always," he said. "And you, young lady; how's my favorite musician?"

"Just fine, sir." Hannah's reply was noticeably formal and lacking emotion.

"Hannah," the man pleaded. "Couldn't I be blessed with just the faintest hint of one of your beautiful smiles?"

Hannah flashed a quick smile that had not the faintest hint of warmth, but the man seemed satisfied.

"Shiloh," Sarah introduced. "This is George Vickers; he and his father own the Slash V. George, this is Shiloh; he has recently come to work on our place."

Vickers turned to acknowledge Shiloh for the first time.

"Have you been told of the trouble on the J H Connected?" he asked.

"I have," Shiloh said softly.

"Then you must be as big a fool as that old mountain man Sarah keeps on her place."

"That is exactly what Caleb told me when I hired on," Shiloh said pleasantly, with a smile that never reached the bleakness in his eyes. "Mrs. Hadley was generous enough to offer me work when I needed a job, so her trouble has become my trouble. Like any cowhand worth his salt, I ride for the brand."

Vickers stared hard at him for fully ten seconds, but Shiloh never blinked or changed his mild expression. Finally, Vickers turned his attention back to Hannah.

"Young lady, are you here for a music lesson this afternoon?" He barely waited for Hannah's nod. "Maybe I'll have a chance to drop by the church and listen to you play. Sarah, I hope you enjoy your meal."

With that, he turned abruptly and returned to his own table where several other men were already eating.

"Sorry, Shiloh," Sarah said. "George has become overly protective of me since Jonathan died."

"Well," Shiloh said quietly. "The Bible does instruct us to look after the widows and orphans."

"Is that what you are doing here, Shiloh?" Sarah asked. "Looking after widows and orphans?"

"Perhaps," Shiloh admitted. "Once before, I couldn't be there when a woman and a boy needed help. Maybe I'm just trying to see that something similar doesn't happen to you and Hannah."

"Thank you, Shiloh," Sarah told him. "Whatever you may have once been in your life, I think you have become a very good man."

"No, ma'am," he said. "I'm just a man trying to serve a very good God."

CHAPTER SEVEN

After dinner, Sarah left to visit friends. Hannah and Shiloh got back into the carriage and started for the church.

"Which way?" Shiloh asked.

"Straight ahead," Hannah told him. "The church is in a grove of trees just beyond the edge of town. "Straight ahead," Hannah told him. "The church is in a grove of trees just beyond the edge of town.

You can hitch the team under the trees between the church and the parsonage, and I'll run over to the house and let Mrs. Reardon know I've arrived. The piano is in the church."

"How far is it from the church to the parsonage?" Shiloh asked. "I can drive you to the parsonage, wait for you to go inside, then drive you and Mrs. Reardon to the church."

"Oh, Shiloh, you cowboys are all the same, you'd ride a horse ten miles to keep from walking ten feet! It's only a few steps between the church and parsonage."

Hannah wrapped both hands around his upper left arm and leaned her head against his shoulder.

"I can't wait to tell Mrs. Reardon what you showed me to do with the chords I can't play!"

"Hannah, have you ever told Mrs. Reardon you were having

trouble or asked her what to do about the chords?"

"No," she said.

"Then maybe you should ask her," he said. "She may actually know a better way, but even if she tells you the same things I did, she *is* your teacher, and it might hurt her feelings to think you had to ask someone else."

"You're right, Shiloh," she agreed. "I was just so excited that I wanted to tell her what I had learned."

"Why don't you tell her what I said about how well you're doing and how well she's taught you?" he asked. "Then she can be pleased for both of you."

"Oh, that's a splendid idea!"

They were just beyond the edge of town when George Vickers rode across the road in front of them and held up his hand for Shiloh to stop.

"Shiloh—is that what Sarah called you?" Vickers asked with an obvious look of disdain.

Shiloh only nodded in reply.

"Why don't you gather whatever few belongings you have and ride south to a warmer climate? We don't need broken down saddle tramps around here."

"It seems that Mrs. Hadley does," Shiloh said. "Someone has to do the work for her, and that old fool of a mountain man can't do it by himself, so I guess she needs an old fool of a saddle tramp."

"You let me worry about Sarah," Vickers said angrily. "You just clear out of this country!"

"Maybe, come spring, I will," Shiloh said. "But it's a little late in the season to be traveling far, and I made the lady a promise I intend to keep."

"You can forget about keeping that promise; you stay around this country and you'll end up dead. You ride out of here while you still can and let me worry about keeping that promise!"

"What will keep you from ending up dead?" Shiloh asked

quietly.

Vickers had no answer. He jerked his horse's head around cruelly, dug in his spurs and galloped down the road away from town, leaving a cloud of dust behind. Shiloh waited until the dust had settled then started the team.

"Shiloh, did you notice that he didn't speak to me?" Hannah asked. "He always makes a big fuss over me in front of Mother, but he ignores me when she isn't around."

"Why do you suppose he does that?"

"Because he wants to marry Mother and thinks fussing over me will make her think he can be a good father."

"Well, you can't blame him for wanting to marry your mother; she is a very beautiful woman and an extraordinarily nice lady," Shiloh said. "But you might want to tell your mother how Vickers acts toward you when she's not around."

"Shiloh, why don't you marry Mother?"

Shiloh turned his head and grinned at her then turned back to watch the road.

"Why would your mother want to marry a broken down old fool of a saddle tramp?"

"You're not old!"

"I'm forty-three."

"Okay, so you *are* old, but Mother is nearly as old as you are."

"Your mother—old?" Shiloh laughed. "She can't be much past twenty-five, that may be old to you, but . . ."

"She's almost thirty-one!" Hannah blurted out.

"She's still a young woman, Hannah," Shiloh said gently. "Maybe you should trust her to do her own matchmaking."

"I won't if she picks George Vickers!"

"Why not? He's a handsome man and a rich one."

"He's a snake in the grass!"

"Well," Shiloh said, as he brought the carriage to a halt beside the church. "This is as good a place as any to pray for him; God *is* in the business of changing lives."

Hannah studied his face.

"You're serious, aren't you?"

"The Bible teaches us to love our enemies and to pray for those who persecute us."

"And I guess God is serious, too?"

"I think that would be a very good guess."

Hannah jumped down from the carriage and ran to get Mrs. Reardon. Once all three were inside the already warm church, and after introductions and the exchange of pleasantries, Shiloh sat unobtrusively on a pew at the back and listened to Hannah's practice. The reverend had walked into town to get a haircut, so Shiloh did not meet him until after the service the next morning.

* * * * * * *

On the front steps of the church, Shiloh followed Sarah and Hannah to shake the hand of the Reverend Timothy Reardon. The man was not large, but neither was he frail. He had a little paunch from recent years of soft living, but he had the strong, meaty hands of the farmer he had been as a younger man. His thinning hair was more gray than black, and his friendly brown eyes crinkled at the corners from years of long days plowing in the sun.

"Welcome, sir," the pastor said. "What did you think of my sermon—always like to get the reactions of someone who has heard me preach for the first time?"

"Well, sir," Shiloh said. "It is, of course, the first time, so I haven't had the benefit of past sermons to know if your subject matter is always so severe—a lot of fire and brimstone in this one—scripturally accurate, but a consistently harsh message."

"Don't you believe the lost should be warned of their fate apart from the salvation of Jesus Christ?"

"Yes, sir, I do," Shiloh agreed. "Even believers need to be reminded from time to time. And Jesus spent a considerable amount of time teaching on the subject. I suppose I am just wondering why you chose not to temper your message with some of the rewards and blessings awaiting those who repent and are saved?"

"A good point, one that I debated within myself while preparing my sermon. I decided there was more than enough material for two sermons—next week I plan to speak on the rewards of salvation. Which sermon do you think is likely to have the greater impact?"

"That I cannot say," Shiloh answered. "Some respond more quickly to fear and others to reward. It may be that the Spirit of God prepared someone this week specifically to hear the topic you chose; next week your message may meet the specific needs of someone else."

"Thank you, Shiloh, it is always my earnest prayer that God is directing my words according to his plan."

"And mine that I am learning to follow His direction," Shiloh told him.

"Then we can both trust that He is faithful to keep His promises." The pastor turned his attention back to Sarah. "I have been given strict instructions to invite you, Hannah and Shiloh to have Sunday dinner with us, and I promise you will find my wife's cooking much superior to anything served at the hotel."

After receiving nodded assents from the other two, Sarah accepted the invitation.

"Hannah and I well know that Ann is a wonderful cook. And you, sir," she said to Shiloh. "Are in for a treat."

CHAPTER EIGHT

The carriage had been parked overnight at the livery, and the horses had been stabled there. Shiloh had gone early to find that the hostler, familiar with the Hadleys weekly routine, had the team hitched and the carriage ready. Shiloh had driven by the hotel for the ladies and the luggage then on to the church. So, after dinner at the Reardons, there was no need to stop for anything on their way through town as he drove them back to the J H Connected. It was late afternoon when they drove up to the front steps of the ranch house, and Caleb was waiting to help the ladies down.

"Did you folks have a good trip?" he asked, as he helped Shiloh carry the luggage into the front room of the house.

"Yes, Caleb, we did," Sarah told him. "I wish you could have come."

"Well, it wouldn't have been wise to leave the ranch without somebody to keep an eye on things, an' Shiloh needed the chance to look over the town an' meet folks. Maybe I'll go next week. I didn't waste the days, though, I managed to catch a mess of trout this afternoon. Got 'em cleaned an' waitin' in a pan of cool water. Figured you'd be mighty tuckered out after the long ride back to the ranch, so I figured I'd fry 'em up fer supper, if you don't mind my meddlin' in yore kitchen."

"That is very thoughtful of you, Caleb," Sarah said. "And much appreciated."

"Are you going to use your lemon flavoring?" Hannah asked.

"Soakin' in it now," Caleb said.

"And dipped in corn meal?"

"Yep."

"Can I help you cook something to go with them?"

"Why don't you think on what you'd like to go with them trout while I ride down to the barn with Shiloh?"

Caleb climbed into the carriage, and Shiloh started the team toward the barn.

"We may be looking for a tall man, after all," Shiloh said and told Caleb the story he had heard from the storekeeper. "And we have some help I hadn't expected, Michael O'Brien from the Slash V rode with me during the war, my top sergeant and as good a man as you'll ever meet."

"Know him from the roundups," Caleb said. "Liked him from the first."

"I'm going to ride to meet him Wednesday morning. By then he'll have had a chance to think over what he knows. Offered to come ride for Mrs. Hadley, but I told him to wait. As much as she needs the help, he may be more valuable where he is for a while."

"If nothing else," Caleb said. "He can keep an eye on that low down mean snake Frank Vickers spawned fer a son."

Shiloh laughed.

"Did you learn that from Hannah?" he asked. "She thinks George plans to marry her mother."

"I ain't liked the way he's looked at Miz Hadley from the first time he seen her—long before the Colonel died," Caleb said. "I trust she has the good judgment to pay him no mind. Just him bein' around gets my hackles raised."

"Well, yesterday he called me a broken down old fool of a saddle tramp and told me to light a shuck—had some similarly flattering words to say about that old fool of a mountain man Mrs.

Hadley keeps on the ranch. I suspect he meant you."

"I 'spect so," Caleb agreed. "Ain't never been no love lost betwixt us."

As they reached the barn, Caleb motioned to the bench behind the house.

"Got a pen fixed in the trees up there and the start of a shelter. Figured to take some saddled horses up after supper."

"Must not be many lazy bones in that skinny old carcass of yours."

"Nary a one."

"While we're at the house for supper, I'd like you to show me that escape tunnel from the cellar, and as we ride out in the morning you can show me where it comes out. Be too dark to see when we take the horses up."

"Remind me," Caleb said. "You mind takin' care of the team while I start them fish to fryin'?"

"Might as well bring some horses into the barn and start getting saddles on them while I'm at it. Any particular horses I ought to get—or avoid?"

"That matched pair of blacks are pers'nal mounts for Miz Hadley an' Hannah. Other than that, I figure a cavalry officer ought to know his way around horseflesh, so use yore own judgment. Ain't really a bad horse on the ranch, the Colonel was mighty partic'lar, 'specially after Hannah got big enough to walk." Caleb got a fond look in his eyes. "She was Miz Busybody herself along about then, disappear in the blink of an eye, headed fer the far horizons. Give us a terrible scare one mornin', took off while we was at breakfast. Found her in a corral full of greenbroke horses, standin' between the front legs of a big mare scratchin' that horse on the underside of her neck. To this day, I'd swear that mare was protectin' Hannah from harm. Let me walk right up an' take the girl from underneath her without so much as flickin' her tail. Only time I was able to get near that horse without throwin' a rope around her neck, even after she was broke to saddle."

"You ever wonder if maybe there was an angel whispering in that mare's ear to keep her still?" Shiloh asked.

"Now that never occurred to me," Caleb said. "But I sure 'nough believe God puts an extry strong motherin' urge in some female critters."

* * * * * * *

That night they feasted on Caleb's fish and Hannah's baked potatoes, then Caleb showed Shiloh how to open the back wall of the root cellar to enter the escape tunnel. The two men examined the entire length of the tunnel, and Shiloh studied the trapdoor at the end very carefully, so he would be able to open it in the dark if necessary.

"There's about six inches of dirt piled on top of the trapdoor," Caleb told him. "We keep a shovel right here at the end of the tunnel to knock the latch beam out an' let the door swing down. A lot of the dirt will likely come down with it, an' you can clear the rest with the shovel. Then up the ladder nailed to the wall beams an' you're out, hopefully free an' clear."

"Okay, I've seen what I needed to see," Shiloh said. "Let's start thinking about a list of supplies for the cave. Might as well pack supplies when we go."

They started with food from the cellar then gathered blankets, suitable outdoor clothing for Sarah and Hannah, cloth for bandages, a few cooking utensils, tin cups and canteens for everyone. Then, from the gunrack and cabinet in the Colonel's study, they took two Spencer carbines, loading tubes, cartridge boxes and cartridges along with four Colt's revolvers, two .45 caliber models, a .38 caliber for Sarah, a .32 caliber for Hannah along with a pair of Winchester 1873 rifles in calibers matching the two smaller Colt's revolvers with cartridges for each.

"I bought some extra cartridges yesterday for my Winchester," Shiloh said. "I'll add a box to this bunch in the morning." He turned to Sarah. "Can you and Hannah shoot?"

"Jonathan bought the .38 caliber Colt and Winchester for me and the .32 caliber guns for Hannah; he taught both of us to use them," she said. "But we have not practiced since he died."

"Then we should probably keep those guns here, so you can practice with them; they can go out through the tunnel with you if you ever have to use it."

"Shiloh," Sarah said. "I have never shot *anything*; I do not know if I could kill a man, even to save my own life."

Shiloh stopped stacking cartridge boxes and looked directly at her.

"Could you kill a man to save Hannah's life?"

"Yes," she said after a moment of hesitation. "I believe I could."

"Keep that thought in mind," he told her. "By shooting a man to save your own life, you might be staying alive to save hers. And if you are ever faced with the necessity to shoot a man, don't hesitate. You may only get one momentary chance before he shoots you."

Shiloh finished stacking the chosen supplies where they could be easily transferred to packsaddles the next morning then he and Caleb led the four saddled horses to the pen Caleb had built in the trees above the house.

"Well, we've made a start," Caleb said as they rode back to the bunkhouse.

"The Colonel made the start with the tunnel," Shiloh reminded him. "But you can almost always make a good plan better. After we've stocked the cave in the morning, maybe we can finish the shelter you've started."

"Then we better get to work on addin' to the stacks of hay and firewood," Caleb said.

"Since there's just two of us to work them, you think it would be a good idea to start pushing the cattle closer in before the first heavy snowfall?"

"I'd say so," Caleb agreed. "An' since you'll be ridin' thataway to meet O'Brien, you might start with that bunch we saw to the north when we was up that way together."

* * * * * * *

The next morning before daylight they took four freshly saddled horses up to the pen and brought the others down. Then they put packsaddles on a pair of mules and their own saddles on the horses they planned to ride that day. When Hannah clanged the triangle, they rode up to the house leading the mules. After breakfast, they set about loading the packsaddles. Once done with that chore, Caleb showed Shiloh the place by a large rock where the escape tunnel ended. Then they rode northeast to the cave, which was in the base of a mountain at the edge of a forested valley.

"Is there another way out of this valley?" Shiloh asked.

"Not one as easy as the way we come in," Caleb told him. "A couple of others by climbin' to the low saddles between some of the peaks."

"Well, break out your lantern and let's see if your she-bear is in there."

Caleb pulled a sack of cotton out of his saddlebags.

"Stuff some of this in yore ears; might keep yore eardrums from bustin' if you have to use that cannon inside the cave."

"You know anything about the inside of the cave?" Shiloh asked.

"Never been inside," Caleb said. "I've been told it's low fer the first ten feet or so then opens up enough fer you to stand. There's an old fire ring of rocks; ceilin' is black from smoke, but the smoke don't build up in the cave, so there must be a crack or hole fer it to rise through. Might be a good idea to light a fire an' see where the smoke comes out, if it does. S'pose to be room on the floor fer eight or ten men to bed down."

"Where's the nearest water?"

"Maybe two hunnerd yards further in there's a creek, an' a brush corral where we used to catch wild horses—may need some repairs, but the creek runs through it, so the penned horses can drink."

"Light the lantern, and I'll see if anyone is home."

Shiloh entered the cave in a low crouch, lantern extended in his left hand, the cocked Winchester in his right. He was back out in less than a minute.

"Well," Shiloh said. "Your lady friend doesn't seem to be at home. You think it's too early for her to be hibernating?"

"Could be," Caleb agreed. "Could also be too much man smell for a bear to choose this cave."

"Riders use this cave a lot?"

"Not often, but our riders all knew it was a place to wait out a storm, whether a summer thunderstorm or a winter blizzard."

"You think it's known to riders from the other ranches?"

"Well, it's likely some of 'em have heard about it. I s'pose it's even possible one or two of 'em have been here, if they was workin' with one of our hands at roundup an' got caught out in the rain. But it ain't likely. Unless they was in danger from a lightnin' strike, most cowboys would just look at rain as somethin' to settle the dust an' cool 'em off a little. Course, they'd complain, an' they'd cuss the mud if the rain lasted long, but it ain't likely they'd seek shelter. A winter blizzard is a whole 'nother matter, but it ain't likely a rider from another ranch would be on our range that time of year."

"I didn't see any sign of bears inside the cave," Shiloh said. "But you might see something I'd miss, so come have a look."

"Ain't likely you missed anythin' I'd see; you found where the killer shot Red from, an' I missed that."

"But I knew to look in the tree, because I'd seen our sharpshooters shoot from trees during the war. And you know bears and bear country a whole lot better than I do."

"Maybe," Caleb said as he followed Shiloh into the cave. "But I doubt it."

After another careful look, both men agreed that it didn't seem likely that bears used the cave.

"Looks like some small critters have been snoopin' around, an' that might be an ol' packrat nest back in the crack in the rock." Caleb said. "But I don't see no bear sign. We've shot some bears fer meat, and we've tried to scare others off the place to keep 'em away from the cattle. But bears have a mind of their own, so there're still plenty of 'em around."

"The canned goods we've brought shouldn't give off food smells to attract any."

The two men spent the next half hour moving the supplies into the cave. They'd cleaned and oiled the firearms before packing them, but they wrapped them and covered them with rocks to keep animals from chewing on the wooden stocks. Then they spent another hour packing in downed limbs for firewood, gathering the wood at a distance from the cave both to leave the near ground undisturbed and to have that wood available in an emergency. While they were gathering wood, Caleb showed Shiloh the creek, catch pen for the horses and the other trails into and out of the valley. They made a few repairs to the catch pen.

"If we have to hole up here," Caleb said when they returned to the cave. "We can cut one of those smaller trees and use it to block wind from blowin' in the mouth of the cave."

"You suggested we build a fire and see if the smoke is visible; I guess now is the time."

They built the fire in the ring of rocks others had used many times before. Then they piled on some green wood and brush to make more smoke than any fire they would be building normally. They watched as the smoke rose straight up to the darkened high ceiling; they could not see a crack or break in the rock, even with the lantern, but the smoke was obviously going out.

"Must be some kind of natural chimney," Caleb said. "Let's go see if we can find where it comes out."

The two men had to ride out away from the cave to be able to see the smoke rising, and they had to climb on foot to reach the place where the smoke was coming out of the rocky ledge above the cave.

"If we keep our fires small an' burn dry wood," Caleb said. "The smoke won't be near as easy to see. Them trees will break it up some, too. Might be more danger from the fire bein' smelled than seen."

"We might try building a teepee of small trees right over the hole to break up the smoke faster," Shiloh suggested. "As long as we don't stop the air from moving, it might help."

"Be worth a try."

"Well, we'll face that if we have to," Shiloh said. "Might as well head back to the house. I made Hannah a couple of promises for the afternoon. I ought to keep them."

Caleb nodded, and they climbed back down to their horses, stopped at the cave to put out the fire and picked up the packmules they had tied in the trees. When they reached the barn, they stripped the saddles off all the animals, then Shiloh caught up his own bay horse, which he had allowed to rest for a couple of days, and, while he was putting his saddle on it, Caleb saddled Hannah's black. Then they rode up to the house and were washing up when Hannah came out to clang the triangle.

"Oh," she said with a hint of disappointment. "You're already here."

"Caleb?" Shiloh asked. "Do you see anyone on this porch?"

"Nobody but Hannah."

"Then I reckon she'd better ring that dinner bell, or the hands won't know it's time to eat."

"Well, I sure hope she rings it," Caleb agreed. "An' soon! Hungry as I am, I'd be plumb put out if she didn't let me know when it was time to eat!"

Hannah gave them the benefit of her brightest smile and

clanged the triangle with obvious delight. After dinner, she held Shiloh to the first promise he had made for the afternoon. Shiloh looked through her sheet music then sat down at the piano.

"Don't expect too much, Hannah," he said. "I haven't touched a piano in several months, and I haven't played regularly for several years."

"I expect the best you are able to do today," Hannah told him, repeating something he had said to her. "No one can expect more from you."

Shiloh smiled up at her, nodded in acknowledgement and began to play Beethoven's "Moonlight" Sonata. If his playing was in any way diminished from lack of practice, his audience of three was unable to detect the flaws. From the soft, slow melody of the opening movement to the final note, Shiloh's performance was brilliant, and they were lost in the music. When he was done, Hannah sat next to him on the piano bench, wrapped her hands around his arm and leaned against his shoulder as she had in the carriage.

"That was truly beautiful, Shiloh," she said. "Will I ever be able to play so well?"

Shiloh wrapped his free arm around her and hugged her.

"I don't see why not," he told her. "You already play better than I did at your age."

"Is that your favorite piece of music?" she asked.

"The opening movement is," he told her. "While it may be musical heresy to say so, there are some parts of the piece that I am not as fond of."

"What parts?" she asked.

"Oh, that's not important, and I wouldn't want my likes or dislikes to shape yours. Hold onto the freedom to form your own opinions. Even if you sometimes have to play music you dislike for the benefit of others, and you should do that in a spirit of giving the best you have to your audience, never lose your personal enjoyment of the music that truly touches you."

"I promise," Hannah told him.

Caleb poked Shiloh in the back with a bony finger.

"I'm plumb glad you rode onto the place," he said. "With a roarin' fire an' you an' Hannah to warm us with yore music, the winter ain't likely to seem so long, nor so bitter."

"Thanks, Caleb."

"That really was 'truly beautiful,'" Sarah told him. "Please feel free to play or practice anytime you wish."

"I will," Shiloh said. "Thank you."

* * * * * * *

Caleb waited on the porch next to Sarah as Shiloh and Hannah rode away from the house.

"Well, ma'am, I ain't quite figured out why he chose to use the name Shiloh. Thought at first it might have been from the Battle of Shiloh during the war, but it don't seem he was at that battle—reckon it's probably from the Bible," Caleb said. "But, puttin' together what Michael O'Brien once told me about the General he rode for, learnin' that Shiloh was the General and O'Brien was his top sergeant, and after hearin' Shiloh play the piano, I reckon now I know who he is. That man ridin' yonder with yore young'un is Brigadier General Paul Daniel Clifton, a genuine war hero of the southern cause an' a concert pianist who once entertained Queen Victoria."

"What would drive a man of such talent and skill to choose obscurity and the hard labor of a cattle ranch to the life he lived?" Sarah asked. "Do you know what happened to him?"

"A little, an' yore husband had the unpleasant duty to be a part of it," Caleb told her. "At the end of the war, just before the surrender at Appomattox Court House, five, well actually it was six, yankee deserters lookin' fer food an' horses found a woman an' her young son alone in the plantation house at Stony Creek, Virginia. Five of the six used an' abused the woman then they killed both the woman an' her boy. The sixth man, a younger brother to the leader of the small group, refused to take part in the crimes an' ran away. He soon came upon yore husband's cavalry on their way to burn the plantation an' told them what was happenin'. They arrived too late to save the woman or the boy. The men were deserters, an' the Colonel was authorized to shoot them on the battlefield; instead, he hung the five an' was inclined to be lenient with the sixth, the young soldier who had run for help. He gave the boy the chance to rejoin his outfit without punishment, but the boy felt such shame for not takin' up arms against the other five, even alone an' outnumbered, that he couldn't accept freedom an' demanded punishment. The Colonel gave the boy a few days to think it over, but he was determined that he should be punished, not freed. So yore husband reluctantly organized a firin' squad an' had him shot. He also completed the original mission before ridin' away and had his men burn the plantation.

"If Shiloh is General Clifton, the woman an' boy were his wife an' son." Caleb said. "The General remained with his regiment an' did his duty until the war ended then he went to Europe an' toured the continent performin' in piano concerts. In England, he was arrested fer public drunkenness, apparently not fer the first time. After he was released, he pretty much vanished off the face of the earth. That was four or five years ago."

"Well, that would explain why he finds it necessary to refrain from strong drink, but it does not tell me why he gave up the piano performances," Sarah said.

"Reckon you'll have to ask him that, Miz Hadley."

"One day, I hope I shall be able to."

CHAPTER NINE

As Hannah led Shiloh into the meadow that was her "favorite place on earth," he immediately understood why. The meadow backed up against the bulk of the Castle Mountains, with Elk Peak visible to the north. On either side, to the east and west, the meadow, no more than a quarter mile in any direction, was surrounded by forested ridges that sloped gently down to the grassland below. A narrow stream tumbled out of the rocks to the north and down a series of small waterfalls into a pool in the rock at the base of the wall; the water flowed out of that first pool down a gentle slope into a series of ever larger pools, each one slightly lower than the one above, then the stream meandered through waist high grass as it slowly flowed out of the small canyon into the short grass beyond. Hannah led him into the trees on the eastern edge of the meadow and reined to a stop behind a huge flat-topped granite boulder. They tied their horses, and she led him in a short, steep climb to the top of the boulder.

"From up here," Hannah told him. "You can see the entire meadow. In the spring, the meadow is filled with wildflowers, and I watched a baby deer, a fawn, being born right at the edge of that lowest pond. I guess I've seen just about every kind of animal in Montana come to drink in this meadow. I think it's kind of funny, sometimes, when I describe a bird I've seen to Caleb and want him to tell me what it is, he can tell me what the Indians call it but not the white man's name."

"That may be because Caleb has spent more years living among Indians than among white men," Shiloh said. "Or it could be because very few white men have seen the birds you have, so the names they've given to them aren't widely known."

"Maybe so," Hannah said. "But either way I still think it's funny, and I like knowing the Indian names."

"Caleb told me hunting parties occasionally ride across the ranch. Have you seen many Indians?"

"Not many. Sometimes, if the hunting was poor, Father would cut out a few steers for them. Last winter some Indians showed up in bad shape. We took care of them, and Mother sent them home with a bunch of cattle. I guess the buffalo herds are getting smaller."

"They are," Shiloh agreed. "A lot of hunters on the plains hunting buffalo for the hides."

"Not for food?"

"No, not for food."

"That's a shame," Hannah said. "Caleb told me that when the plains Indians kill a buffalo they use just about all of it, for food, for their teepees, even for their bowstrings. What will happen to the Indians when the buffalo are gone?"

"I don't know, Hannah. Eventually, they'll likely all end up on reservations. Last January, the government gave orders to move all the tribes onto reservations, and the Army is trying to carry out those orders. The Cherokees, down in the Indian Territory, are doing fairly well, but they were already living at peace, fully adapted to our ways, before they were forced to move west on the 'Trail of Tears.' Some of the tribes may not do so well. And none of them want to give up their free way of living for reservation life. That's why so many tribes fought together against Crook at the Rosebud and Custer on the Little Big Horn this past summer."

"My father knew Custer, but I don't think he liked him." Hannah said. "I wonder what Father would have thought of Custer's last battle."

"The commanding officer almost always gets the glory in victory or takes the blame in defeat, but it's usually the success or failure of his subordinates to carry out his orders or to adapt to the unexpected that determines which way a battle goes. I fought against Custer; he was bold and daring, many thought him to be a fool. I know he was despised by Southerners, and I've heard that Union soldiers had no love for him. Most of the stories coming out of the Little Big Horn make him out to be an arrogant fool, but there is probably more to the story than we've heard, more than we may ever hear."

"You said you never actually met my father, even though you often fought against him. If you had met him, do you think you would have liked him?"

"Hannah, I've never heard a single uncomplimentary word spoken about your father," Shiloh said. "I think I would have liked him very much."

"I know he would have liked you."

"Thank you, Hannah, that means a lot to me."

The two of them spent the late afternoon sitting next to each other on that huge boulder, sometimes talking, sometimes quietly watching as a parade of wildlife drifted into and out of the meadow, stopping to drink, to browse or graze, to rest in the tall grass beneath the bright sun and the big sky. Finally, as the sun was sinking toward the western ridge, Shiloh told Hannah it was time to start back, and they climbed down off of the boulder and mounted their horses. They rode side by side out of the trees and along the eastern edge of the meadow. Hannah stopped abruptly, and Shiloh's horse took another step before Shiloh stopped him.

"Shiloh," Hannah whispered. "Look!"

As Shiloh turned to see what Hannah had seen, he saw a sudden flash from the trees below the setting sun and threw himself backwards from his saddle; he heard the bullet as he fell, but he had already landed in a heap, his impact softened somewhat by the tall, thick grass, when he heard the report of the rifle.

"Shiloh!" Hannah screamed, jumped down from her saddle and ran to him.

"Hannah," he whispered as she dropped to her knees beside him. "I'm okay; the bullet missed, your call saved me. But I want him to think I'm dead, so I need you to do some playacting."

She fell on top of him and hugged him then whispered back to him.

"What do you want me to do?"

"I want you to roll me onto my back—downhill, I won't be able to help you—he's probably still watching. I'm counting on that. Then straighten my legs, fold my arms and lay my hands on my chest, left hand first, right hand next and unfasten the flap on my pistol holster before you get up, then go find my hat and come back to exactly where you are—you're between me and the rifleman. As you kneel down again, I'm going to draw my revolver, and I want you to cover it by laying my hat on my chest."

"Okay, here goes."

Hannah pushed herself up and acted as if she was trying to roll him toward herself, then she stood and stepped over him to the downhill side. She straightened his arms and legs then rolled him onto his back. After she had straightened his legs again, she moved back to the uphill side, folded his left arm with her right hand while she unfastened the holster, which he wore on his left side for a cross draw, with her left hand. Then she reached across and placed his right hand on top of his left. It took her a little while to find his hat in the tall grass, then she returned with it as he had told her and covered his movement with her body and the hat as he reached across and drew his revolver from its holster. After she had positioned the hat over the drawn pistol, she bent over and kissed him on the forehead.

"You did very well, Hannah," he whispered. "Now get on your

horse, leave mine and ride out of here as fast as you safely can. Tell Caleb what's happened and that if all goes well I'll be back to the ranch house a couple of hours after dark."

"I love you, Shiloh."

"I love you, too, Hannah," he whispered. "Now go! I don't think he would harm you, but he's had plenty of time to reload that rifle by now, so let's not tempt him."

Hannah squeezed his shoulder, stood up, ran to her horse and rode away at a gallop.

"*Now, Mister Sharpshooter*," Shiloh thought. "*You didn't ride down to check on any of the others, but I doubt that you can see me in this tall grass; let's see if you come down to make sure I'm dead.*"

Shiloh remained still until it had been fully dark for more than an hour, trusting his horse, which he could hear cropping grass nearby, to warn him of the arrival of any threat. Finally, he rose silently from the ground, stepped into the saddle and walked the horse quietly out of the meadow. Then he nudged the bay up to a canter and rode straight for the barn. Caleb was waiting at the door of the darkened barn and swung the door shut behind Shiloh as he rode in. Then he lit a lantern.

"Hannah get back without any trouble?" Shiloh asked.

"Had her horse lathered some an' mighty excited herself, but she was fine—just worried about you."

"Well, she probably saved my life. We were riding out of the valley side-by-side when she stopped for something. I stopped a step or two later, which gave the killer a clear shot at me. Then Hannah whispered for me to look at something, and as I turned to see what it was I caught the muzzle flash out of the corner of my eye. He was far enough away that I managed to throw myself out of the saddle before the bullet hit me. I was already on the ground playing dead when I heard the crack of the rifle. I don't know what Hannah wanted me to look at, but her call saved my life."

"Herd of elk," Caleb told him. "She saw 'em comin' out of the trees, said there was a big ol' bull leadin' 'em, an' she wanted you to see him."

"You'd of been proud of her, Caleb," Shiloh said. "I was. She did the smoothest bit of playacting I've ever seen—did several things on her own that made it more believable. But the sharpshooter never came down to make sure I was dead, just like the others."

"You plan to stay dead fer a while?"

"Seems like a good idea. How long was it before you got into town to report the others?"

"A day or two after they was shot, dependin' on when an' where they was found."

"Did you take the bodies to town?"

"Nope, buried 'em here an' went in to report it. Preacher came out a few days after and gave a service for each one."

"Who all came to the funerals?" Shiloh asked.

"Besides our own people, the preacher an' his wife, Jenkins, the storekeeper, come to all three, an' I think maybe one of his bartenders, that big negro they call Smoke come to all three—I'm sure he was at Jim's an' Tom's, not so sure about Red's. That friend of yours, O'Brien was at Red's an' Jim's; I don't know that he was even in this part of the country when Tom was shot. He come with Frank an' George Vickers; they was at all three. Not many others come to Tom's or Red's, maybe one or two cowboys from neighborin' ranches. Nearly everybody in the country come to Jim's funeral; he was well-known and well-liked, prob'ly as many folks come fer his as fer the Colonel's. You wonderin' if maybe the killer was among those who come?"

"Just a thought, maybe not a good one," Shiloh admitted.

"You want me to go into town tomorrow an' report you dead?"

"The day after tomorrow, while I ride out to talk to O'Brien. Tomorrow, we can dig a shallow grave and pile rocks on it to match the others then put up a marker. And we can finish that shelter you've started for the horses. . ."

"I done that this afternoon while you was off gettin' yourself shot at," Caleb said dryly.

"Well, then we can ride out and look at where the shot came from, see if the killer left anything for us to find."

"That ain't likely," Caleb said.

"No, but we should look just in case."

Shiloh had unsaddled his horse and rubbed him down while they were talking; he put his horse in a stall and his saddle in the tackroom then Caleb turned out the lantern and opened the barn door.

"Miz Hadley has some supper fer you in the warmin' oven on the stove, an' they'll both want to know you're back safe, so you might as well go on up. Figured you might be plannin' to lay low fer a while, so I told 'em to leave the front of the house dark in case anybody was watchin' to see if you come back alive. Figured they'd expect you to wash up on the back porch an' go in through the kitchen like we usually do. So go in through the front door. I've done et, so I'm goin' to bed. See you at breakfast."

"Goodnight then," Shiloh told him.

At the front door of the house, Shiloh knocked lightly and the door swung inward immediately. He stepped inside and the door closed just as quickly. Then Hannah wrapped her arms around his waist and buried her face in his vest.

"Oh, Shiloh," she said. "I was so worried about you!"

"I'm fine, Hannah," he told her. "And I'm mighty proud of you and mighty grateful. You saved my life."

"It might have been that big, beautiful bull elk that saved you, but it wasn't me. I didn't know someone was going to shoot at you. Maybe God sent that elk to get my attention just at the right time."

"Maybe so, but thanks just the same."

"Come on, Mother's in the kitchen putting your supper on the table. She'll want to see that you're alright."

In the kitchen, Shiloh assured Sarah that he was unharmed and retold the story with much emphasis on Hannah's playacting performance. Sarah allowed Hannah to stay up while Shiloh ate then told her to go to bed. After a hug for Shiloh, Hannah reluctantly obeyed.

"Would you wait, Shiloh, while I tell her goodnight and turn out her lamp?"

"Of course," he said. "And take your time with Hannah. I'm in no hurry."

Sarah was gone only a few minutes.

"Shiloh, would you like to sit out in the porch swing?" she asked. "It is warm enough tonight, and we shall be able to talk without our talk keeping Hannah awake."

"Yes, I'd like that," he said and followed her to the swing.

"I love sitting out here in the evening," she said. "The moonlight on the water is beautiful, the stars are brilliant, and I love to listen to the sounds of the night."

"Some nights, during the war, I'd try to find a quiet place where I could relax, listen to the night sounds and look at the stars," Shiloh told her. "But most often, I was concerned that the night sounds might be northern troops creeping up on our encampment."

"Jonathan rarely talked to me about the war; it seemed to be a subject that he was only comfortable discussing with the men who served with him. Sometimes, he would have nightmares that I knew from his mumblings were about the war, but he would never talk about them. I never understood that; I was his wife. Why would he not confide in me?"

"War is almost always portrayed in heroic deeds, Mrs. Hadley, but seldom is the terror and horror of war truthfully expressed, nor can it be adequately. Unless a person has seen war, lived it, survived it, he or she has great difficulty in understanding what a soldier has done or why. Your husband may have been afraid you would be shocked or appalled by actions he took almost daily, but, more likely, he would have wanted to spare you the pain of visualizing the terrible images of war."

"But why do men go to war?" she asked. "Why was this war necessary? I believed that slavery was wrong, but was war the only way to free the slaves? Why did you go to war, Shiloh? You owned a plantation. Were you fighting to keep slaves?"

"I think men go to war because it is in their nature. A man would willingly give up his life for his wife, his children, his family. And men are taught from childhood to have that same sense of duty and responsibility toward community and country; they feel bound by their very manhood to honor the call to defend what they believe. God created us to be spiritual warriors, and one of the last instructions Jesus gave was to carry a sword," Shiloh said. "But I don't believe this war was truly necessary; it became inevitable when the political leaders of both sides were unable to reconcile their differences. I believe the south was correct that the federal government had no constitutional right to infringe on rights reserved for the individual States. And the desire to preserve States' rights was stronger in many southerners than the desire to keep slaves. Slavery was the political issue used to promote support for the war in the north, and many in the south supported slavery, even though most of them did not own slaves. But slavery would have collapsed of its own weight in time; it simply wasn't profitable, and many of the largest slaveholders had or were beginning to realize that. In Virginia, long before the war, our House of Delegates came within one vote of abolishing slavery. And I had freed the slaves I inherited two years before the war began."

"You freed them?" Sarah asked. "You did not sell them to at least recover their monetary value?"

"I freed them."

"Why?"

"Partly, I freed them because it was too costly to support them as slaves, and I didn't sell them, because I still needed them to do the work. But those are only the business reasons for what I did, and those are the realities that would have eventually brought slavery to an end in the south," Shiloh told her. "But I guess I'd have to go back to my childhood to explain fully the personal reasons I felt obligated to free the slaves I owned.

"When I was born, my mother selected a young negro mother to serve as my mammy. I'm not certain when in history the practice started or why, perhaps it started when a new mother didn't have enough milk to feed her baby. But it became commonplace in the south, and it may have been more for convenience and vanity than of necessity in most families. The young mother was called Penny, because my mother said she was only worth a penny, and she raised me. She was the only adult who ever showed me affection as a child. Oh, I remember times when my mother would show me off to the ladies who came to visit, as my father would parade me in front of his friends. And there were probably times before I was old enough to remember that one or the other picked me up or carried me, but neither ever truly gave me love. Yet Penny accepted her duties joyfully, and displayed as much love and affection for me as she did for her daughter Daisy. I never remember a time that she failed to greet me with a hug and a kiss. I wouldn't have known what love was had she not shown me, and I loved her. Penny was a slave, a servant, yet she was the kindest, sweetest person I knew. And she was extremely intelligent. She knew dozens of stories, poems and songs, and she seemed to have the Bible memorized—quite an extraordinary feat for a young negro mother when it was forbidden by my father to teach any of our slaves to read."

"Wasn't it against the law to teach slaves to read?" Sarah asked.

"Not in Virginia," Shiloh explained. "It may have been in a few southern States, but I don't know that to be true. It may have been northern propaganda."

"You think we were lied to in the north?" she asked.

"You may have been about some things, and we probably were, too," he admitted.

"What a shame," Sarah said. "But I've interrupted your story, please continue."

"When I was nine, it was decided that I should go to boarding school, a boys' military academy, to prepare me for the responsibilities of manhood. Penny was no longer needed, so she was sold. She was sold partly because she was pregnant again, and a close friend of my mother's was also pregnant and would need a nanny shortly after Penny was due to deliver her baby. But I think partly she was sold because my mother was jealous of my affections for her. Daisy was not sold, neither was Jimbo, the field slave that Penny had married in the only way that was allowed on our farm, by exchanging vows with God as their witness.

"When I was told Penny had been sold, I cried, pleaded, begged, pitched tantrums, refused to eat. I told my mother that I loved Penny, and I didn't want her to be sold. I was told it wasn't right for me to love a slave. I argued that I had a horse, and it was alright for me to love my horse, even if the horse didn't seem love me back. And I had a useless hound that followed me everywhere and loved me as much as I loved him, and that was alright. Why was it wrong for me to love Penny, when she loved me back the same way my dog did? I used every weapon I had in my arsenal to win that battle and get Penny back, but I lost. Penny was sold, and I went off to school.

"At the academy, I learned that the way my father did things, the way he handled our slaves, was not the common practice in Virginia, and I realized that we were actually held in low regard for it by most of our neighbors. Learning from others that their slaves were educated, that they were allowed to marry, and that families were not separated when sold, caused me great shame and created constant friction as I grew strong in my convictions and argued with my father.

"My father died suddenly when I was seventeen, and I was brought home from school permanently to assume the responsibilities as his only heir. I began immediately to make changes. My slaves were allowed to marry, and I hired a minister both to hold services and to teach them to read. I had the good fortune to be guided by an elderly neighbor, a wise man and a man who had already realized that it would profit him more to free his slaves then hire them to work for him, than it would to keep them in bondage. I don't know that I understood in the beginning why I was so pleased to discover that there were sound financial reasons to free my slaves, but it became clear to me some weeks after I returned from school."

Shiloh paused for a moment, easing his legs into a more comfortable stretch and rubbing the back of his neck with his left hand. He was looking out at the moon reflecting off of the beaver pond, but he was seeing only the images in his mind.

"I was riding in one of the fields one morning when I happened to recognize Jimbo talking to a slave from a neighboring plantation. That slave passed something to Jimbo, and it was obvious to me that they were trying hard not to be discovered. I couldn't imagine at the moment what they were hiding, but I decided I needed to find out. As the other slave drove off in a wagon on his master's business, I rode up to Jimbo.

"Jimbo greeted me with a broad smile, 'Ain't it a pleasant mornin', Massuh?' And I agreed that it was. Then I asked him what the other slave had given him. I've never been certain what I saw in his eyes at that moment, but he looked directly at me, something our slaves were taught not to do, and handed me a folded paper. 'It's a letter fum mah Penny, Massuh.' 'Can you read, Jimbo?' I asked. 'Nah, Massuh, Ah cain't read; a man reads 'em to me an' writes whut Ah tell him to say. Mah Penny ken read, Massuh; you done taught her when you wuz a little boy, wifout eben knowin' you wuz doin' it.'

"I found out then that when I was learning to read and Penny was pretending to drill me in my lessons, she was actually having me teach her to read. She did it so skillfully that I was never aware of what she was doing. At that age, I probably just accepted that as an adult she should be able to read. But I taught her the alphabet by reciting the letters while she pointed to them, then I taught her words by reading aloud to her or reciting verses she'd had me memorize while she followed along in the book the verse was from. She would ask me what a word meant, as if she knew and was testing me, and I would tell her. In that way, I taught her to read. Then she taught herself to write by watching how I formed the letters. I was amazed when Jimbo told me.

"'Would you like me to read her letter to you, Jimbo?' I asked, and it surprised both of us that I offered. 'Ah'd shore 'preciate that, Massuh.' Jimbo told me.

"So I read the letter to him. Penny told him how their son Tommy was doing; Jimbo had never seen Tommy, even though he and Penny lived on a plantation that was less than twenty miles away. Penny was teaching the eight-year-old skills that would make him useful as a house servant, hoping to keep him from the hard labor of the fields. She asked about Daisy, whom she hadn't seen since being sold. She reminded him that she and Tommy prayed for him and for Daisy every day and asked that he and Daisy do the same for them. Then she told him that she was concerned for her future. She had learned that her young charge was being sent off to school in the fall, as I had been. She was afraid that she might be sold again, and she was worried about Tommy and what would happen to him if they were separated.

"Some time earlier in my life, I had finally become resolved to the idea that I should never see Penny again. Her letter broke my heart. I handed it to Jimbo, mounted my horse and rode away without another word, without giving him the slightest hint of what I planned to do. I rode straight to the Jackson plantation and bought both Penny and Tommy, borrowed a carriage and drove them back to Stony Creek. It was well past midnight when I helped them out of the carriage in front of the shanty where Jimbo and Daisy lived, but lanterns were hurriedly lit and a father met his son, a brother met his father and his sister. I left them together, thanking me and praising God. Penny hugged me, as she had always hugged me, as she had spontaneously hugged me at the Jackson plantation before she had any idea of why I was there. Before I left, I promised them that I had a plan and that they would be freed that very day."

Shiloh turned to look at Sarah, seeking understanding and finding it in her silent nod.

"I kept that promise. I drove the carriage on to the plantation house, turned it over to a sleepy-eyed servant to look after the horse, and went straight to the office I had inherited from my father. Before I retired for the night, I had written papers giving four slaves the freedom to become a family. They were the first, and it took eight years for me to free all of my slaves. Where possible, I bought and freed family members my father had sold. Sadly, I couldn't trace them all."

Shiloh finished the story without interruption, looking off into the distance and the darkness. When he turned again to Sarah, he found her face glowing in the moonlight with tears streaming down her cheeks.

"How many did you free?" she asked.

"I inherited 76 slaves from my father; counting those I bought back, I freed 82."

"And it profited you in the end to do it?"

"Until the war. When the south surrendered, I would have lost it all. By the beginning of the war, I had the former slaves farming parcels of land on shares. To try to keep the land from being stolen by carpetbaggers, I deeded the parcels to the tenants and gave them the tools and animals that didn't already belong to them. Some have lost the land I gave them, but many are prospering. I don't know if the bitterness and pain and prejudice will ever heal completely in this life. I doubt it. But I did all that I could do; I gave all that I had to give."

"Shiloh, would you mind telling me about your wife and son?"

He was startled, and he could not conceal it.

"How do you know about them?"

"Caleb figured out who you were and told me what he knew about you, about the part my husband played in your tragedy. We had agreed to let you tell us what you wanted us to know in your own good time. And I suppose I should not have asked, but I remember how much it hurt to lose Jonathan. After the story you have just told me, I guess I thought maybe I could help you with your grief."

"Thank you for your concern, and perhaps you can help, but the story you've just heard was difficult enough to tell. You are only the second person to hear it. I don't think I'm up to talking about my wife or son tonight. Ask me again another night."

"I shall."

CHAPTER TEN

Well before daylight the next morning, Shiloh and Caleb were up working in the barn.

"After you ride out to talk to yore friend, an' I ride to town to tell folks yore dead, maybe we can get on with cuttin' wood an' hay," Caleb said. "Course, that'll likely get interrupted by yore funeral. Leastways, won't nobody be expectin' us to have close feelin's fer you, you bein' so new to the country an' all, so I won't have to pretend to be put out at yore passin', but I shore wish you'd be more careful to stay alive—diggin' graves an' makin' markers is a heap of work. An' I've sorta begun to take a likin' to you—be upsettin' to have to bury you a second time."

"Well, I appreciate how much you have to do around the place," Shiloh told him, as he cinched the saddle on the fourth horse. "So I'll try not to add to your burden by getting myself killed permanently dead. You want to lead these horses outside after I turn out the lantern and open the barn door?"

Caleb mounted the horse he had just finished saddling and took the reins of the other three as Shiloh brought them alongside. Then Shiloh put out the lantern, opened the door long enough for Caleb to get out with the horses and closed the door after them. Once Shiloh was mounted, the two men rode in silence up to the hidden pen on the bench, switched out the horses and rode back to the barn. After unsaddling those four and putting away the tack, they brought out their own rigs, released the four horses they had brought down, caught up a grulla that was Caleb's favorite of the string he rode and a buckskin he had suggested as a likely horse for the string Shiloh was putting together for himself.

"I think I'll leave this buckskin in the barn and walk up to the house for breakfast," Shiloh said. "You go ahead and ride up like you usually do. If anyone is watching this morning, it might keep our deception believable a while longer. We'll just have to hope anyone watching sees enough at first light not to stick around long. If he's still watching when we come out from breakfast, he'll know he missed."

"You given any thought to why I ain't been shot at?" Caleb asked.

"Some," Shiloh admitted. "Only two things I've come up with—one, the killer doesn't consider you a threat to whatever his plan is or, two, he figures Mrs. Hadley and Hannah will need you with them once he forces them off the place. I don't think he means to harm them unless he becomes convinced there is no other way to get rid of them."

"There ain't, but let's hope we can catch him before he figures that out," Caleb said. "I think he's smart enough to know that if he starts shootin' ladies an' little girls, the territorial marshal that ain't got around to lookin' fer him is likely to come at a gallop. But uncommonly smart folks can be uncommonly stupid when things don't go the way they think they should. An' I ain't figured out why, if he wants this place so bad, that he didn't just shoot Miz Hadley first and be done with the killin'."

"Well, I've known some men who would have done just that," Shiloh admitted. "But even among bad men, men who would kill you or me without remorse, some have a code of honor strong enough to keep them from harming a woman or a child."

The two men spent the morning digging a false grave and

examining the slope above the meadow where the sharpshooter had fired from. They found very little and learned nothing new about their adversary. They spent the afternoon moving cattle closer to the ranch headquarters. Once they released the gathered bunch to graze on new grass, the two men turned their horses toward the barn.

"Caleb, did you grow up in the west?" Shiloh asked.

"Well, sort of," he said. "My pa couldn't stand crowded places. As the frontier moved west, he moved with it. I was born in Kentucky, but as settlers moved in around us, Pa would sell out, move farther west an' build ag'in. I reckon the only thing that kept Ma sane was the fact that Pa's best friend married Ma's sister, an' ever'time we moved, they moved with us. We spent most of the time I was a boy livin' in one log cabin or another on the banks of the Ohio then we follered the Mississippi north into the Minnesota country. When my older brother an' me was in our teens, we backtracked to the Missouri an' moved west as far as St. Joe. By that time, Pa an' Uncle Jim was gettin' wore down some with age, back then I figured they was already old men, so they settled permanent an' opened a tradin' post. Ma an' Aunt Mary figured it was about time."

"I bet they did," Shiloh agreed with a grin. "What did you do after that?"

"Oh, one thing an' another," Caleb told him. "Aaron, my brother, an' me spent two years as teamsters on the Santa Fe Trail an' another dozen or so trappin' beaver in the Rockies. Then we went to scoutin' an' huntin' fer wagon trains headed to California an' Oregon. The last trip we made together nearly got us killed, an' Aaron found a wife on that trip, so he stayed in Oregon."

"I would have thought you could end up dead most any day on the trail," Shiloh observed. "What made that last trip so dangerous?"

"I reckon we had lots of close calls over the years, but we did somethin' plumb stupid on that trip. Didn't really have no choice in the matter, a missionary family had to make repairs to a broken down wagon, slid into a deep rut an' broke the two wheels on the right side an' the back axle. The captain of the wagon train was afeared to wait on them, afeared of gettin' caught in the mountains by an early snow. So he up an' left 'em to fend fer theirselves. Aaron was already sweet on the missionary's oldest daughter by that time, so he weren't plannin' on goin' nowhere without that girl. I reckon I couldn't've left 'em nohow, but I shore weren't leavin' Aaron to help them by hisself. Them folks didn't know nuthin' they needed to know to keep 'em alive, an' it was at least a three day ride to the nearest place we knew there was trees fer wood to fix the wagon.

"I didn't know the Lord yet when I rode off from that busted wagon alone to find wood, but, lookin' back on it, He must've had a plan for all of us even then. About a half day out, I come across another busted wagon that somebody had abandoned. There was enough left of it that I was able to salvage what we had to have an' get back that same night. We had the missionary's wagon rollin' by noon the next day an' pushed hard fer most of a week to catch up to that wagon train. We was about half a day ahead of a Kiowa huntin' party when we found the wagon train. If them Kiowa had caught up to us when we was by ourselves, we'd of most likely lost our scalps. Instead, them missionary folks led me an' Aaron to the Lord. I stayed in Oregon long enough to help Aaron get a cabin built fer his new bride, then I headed fer the gold fields of California."

"Did you ever strike gold?" Shiloh asked.

"Never enough in one place to make it worth the diggin'. Did better supplyin' meat to the miners an' drivin' freight wagons from the ships to the boomtowns. Finally caught one of them ships bound fer the Carolinas." Caleb grinned ruefully. "Reckon that was an experience worth the doin' oncet, but it shore taught me I weren't cut out to be no sailor."

"How did you meet Jonathan Hadley?"

"After I got off that ship in Charleston, I made my way back west to St. Joe to see my folks. While I was there, some men workin' fer Thomas Hadley come to see me about guidin' a huntin' trip fer a Russian baron Mr. Hadley was entertainin'. The pay was good, so I hired on. If I'd had any idea what they meant to do, I would've run from the job. It took three wagons just to carry the baggage of Baron Gregor Rostov, another wagon fer his chef an' the silver servin's fer the meals. We had enough silver along to attract all the riffraff on the plains. Worse'n that, the baron had heard about the Black Hills from somebody an' was determined to hunt there. I couldn't make him understand what 'sacred ground' meant to most ever' Injun tribe I've even heard about. So I finally just said no an' let Thomas Hadley fix it by usin' the excuse that we couldn't travel that far an' get back before winter set in."

"Where did you end up taking them?" Shiloh asked, as they rode up to the barn.

"Southwest a ways out on the Santa Fe trail to a place I knew had good water. Once we set up camp an' the baron shot a buffalo, ever'thin' went purty well. Jonathan Hadley was just a boy then, but he shadowed me ever'where I went that whole trip, an' I did other jobs fer his pappy over the years. Reckon that's why he asked me to come out here with his Uncle Ed."

"Did you ever get back to Oregon to see your brother?"

"Nope, an' neither of us ever learned to read nor write, so we didn't send many letters. His wife would write when she knew where to send mail. They built a fine farm in the Willamette Valley an' raised three boys an' two girls. Aaron went to be with the Lord about three years ago. Annabelle follered him less than a year later. Reckon they'll have to introduce me to their children when I catch up to them in heaven."

"I'm looking forward to seeing quite a few lost friends and family members myself. I lost my wife and young son toward the end of the war," Shiloh told him. "Worst part is, I've lost too many that might not be there, most of them before I knew how to map out the way."

"Me, too," Caleb agreed sadly. "Me, too."

They reached the ranch headquarters early for supper, so, after they turned out their horses, Shiloh began to teach Caleb to recite and write the alphabet. Caleb learned quickly and had made good progress when they heard Hannah clang the triangle.

* * * * * * *

"Mrs. Hadley, how did you meet your husband?" Shiloh asked when they were alone after supper. "Had you known him long before you married?"

"Actually, I knew who he was for years before he ever spoke to me," she said. "My family lived in Saratoga Springs, in New York, and my grandfather managed a lodge on Great Sacadaga Lake on the edge of the Adirondacks. For as far back as I can remember, I spent my childhood summers helping my grandfather at the lodge. The Hadleys came to the lodge every summer, so I knew who Jonathan was long before I actually knew him."

"What kind of work did you do for your grandfather?" Shiloh asked.

"Whatever was needed of me that I was physically able to do. I started out sweeping and cleaning in the lodge. As I grew older I served food and cleaned up after the meals and made beds and tidied up the rooms. I even cleaned the outhouses a few times one summer when my grandfather was older—not just the insides, but the undersides as well—until Gwumps was able to hire a man to take care of that as part of his other outside duties. Gwumps was as close as I could come to Gramps when I was a toddler; my grandfather thought it was cute; my grandmother thought it was accurate, and the name stuck."

"What happened that allowed a young man of the aristocracy to be introduced to the hired help?" Shiloh asked. "If a young man of my station had shown any interest in a girl of lesser station, it would have been cause for tactful but stern discipline on most plantations. In private, it would have been more stern than tactful where my parents were concerned."

"Well, actually, Jonathan and I were never formally introduced," she said then she laughed. "And he had invited me to a ball before he found out that I was not a guest at the lodge, then his sense of chivalry prevented him from withdrawing the invitation, but I am getting ahead of my story."

"It may have had more to do with your beauty than his chivalry," Shiloh suggested. "But he obviously had more courage and boldness than I would have had as a young man. I dealt with men as an equal by the time I was twelve or thirteen, but I was scared to death of women and girls well into my twenties or early thirties."

"I accept your compliment," she said. "But I honestly cannot imagine you being afraid of anything."

"I may have hidden it well, but I was terrified of talking to most young ladies. I knew fear in the face of battle during the war, any man who claims otherwise is either a liar or a fool—courage isn't the absence of fear, it is the ability to do your duty in spite of fear, and controlled fear can prevent foolish behavior. Yet I may well have been more afraid of conversation with a young lady than of exchanging sword strokes and bullets with yankee cavalry. But, I have interrupted your story, please forgive me and continue. How did you find yourself on speaking terms with the aristocracy?"

"I have always loved being outdoors, so it was my habit when I had time off from my duties to paddle a canoe away from the lodge to some distant shore of the lake and hike into the mountains. I was returning to the canoe from one such hike when I nearly stumbled across Jonathan and his best friend, Benjamin Franklin Adams. Ben had twisted his ankle, and I stopped to offer help. I looked anything but a young lady at the time. I was dressed for the woods in boots, men's britches, a flannel shirt, a floppy brimmed hat, wearing a loaded knapsack and carrying a canteen," she laughed at the picture of herself. "Horror of horrors, I was even perspiring."

"Very unladylike," Shiloh agreed.

"Neither of them noticed. Ben was in quite a bit of pain, and Jonathan was trying to decide what to do about it. Ben was a few inches taller and a good many pounds heavier than Jonathan, even as a younger man or boy, so it was decided that it would be imprudent for Jonathan to attempt to carry him several miles back to the lodge, especially since both of them also had knapsacks and canteens, and each of them carried a revolver. When I arrived and told them I had a canoe close by and could paddle it to within fifty yards of where they were on the trail, the issue was resolved. I gave them directions to the lakeshore; neither of them was competent at that time to stray from the beaten path without getting lost. Jonathan would support most of Ben's weight while he hobbled to the water's edge, and I would bring the canoe to them.

"Both balked when I picked up Ben's knapsack along with my own to carry them to the canoe, so I left Ben's for them to carry in order not to wound their pride any more than was necessary. Actually, Ben's knapsack weighed less than mine and had very little in the way of useful equipment among the contents, as I had discovered while searching it for anything I could use to wrap his ankle. These were two city boys playing at being woodsmen. Jonathan became a skilled woodsman during the war; Ben was killed at his side during a skirmish at Rappahannock Station early in the war, so he probably never had the opportunity.

"When I reached the shore with the canoe, I nosed in at a shallow angle to make it easier for them to get in, but I stayed in my place and steadied the canoe with a paddle brace to avoid a confrontation over who was going to do most of the steering. I was actually impressed at the grace with which Jonathan took instruction from a girl—I was barely fifteen at the time—and that he admitted he had never paddled a canoe before. We managed to reach the shore at the lodge without either of them capsizing us; Jonathan and I left Ben on a bench by the lake and went in search of a carriage to transport him.

"I was no longer needed from that point and attempted to say goodbye. Before he even knew my name, Jonathan invited me to be his guest at the ball to be held later in the week. When I explained that I was employed by the lodge rather than being a guest there and that I had no suitable clothes for such an event, he quickly decided that I was about the same size as his sister, told me that she had more clothes than she could ever wear and insisted that I come with him to meet her.

"I had too many times been on the receiving end of overly polite but very condescending remarks made by rich young ladies who snickered afterwards to each other at their cleverness and my supposed ignorance of their rude intent to keep me in my place, so I was quite reluctant to subject myself to more of the same from Jonathan's sister. Still, I did find him both appealing and interesting, and, while he was certainly arrogant in many ways, he seemed not the least concerned that I was as 'dirt poor' as I appeared when we met on the trail, and I really did think it would be nice to attend at least one ball at some point in my life. So I allowed myself to be persuaded into accompanying him to his family's quarters to meet his sister.

"Clara was some ten years older than I, seemed not the least put out with her brother's demand that she find suitable clothing for me, and if she was anything but delighted to meet me I was never able to detect such negative feelings in her words or manner. We quickly became friends; over the years, I have come to regard her as the dear sister I never had growing up.

"What Jonathan intended to be a 'whirlwind' romance ending in an early marriage was soon postponed by growing rumors of war. His honor would not allow him to put me at great risk of becoming a young widow, so he promised that he would endeavor not to be so foolish as to get himself killed and asked me to wait for him to return. I did so willingly and would have married him before he left to do battle, since I knew I would suffer from worry in any event.

"During the war, I frequently stayed with his family; his parents accepted me as readily as did Clara. Perhaps I wrongly judged all wealthy people by the actions of a few young girls who slighted me at the lodge, but I am more inclined to believe that their devout belief in the Savior instilled a degree of humility in the Hadleys that I often found lacking in people of their wealth and status. Jonathan and I were married the very week he returned from the war."

"What brought you west to a cattle ranch?" Shiloh asked. "The Hadleys have many business interests, any one of which could have become a place for Jonathan to contribute, if he felt the need, but none of them involve livestock."

"Jonathan was already planning to move west before the war—he looked forward to the adventure. But the war changed him," she told Shiloh. "On the one hand he had seen and inflicted much hardship on civilians; he had seen real hunger among the civilian populace and the soldiers he fought against—he even went hungry a few times along with his own men when shipments of supplies were delayed or disrupted. But he had also learned to love living and working in the outdoors. Perhaps, you can understand that, having lived under similar and perhaps more difficult conditions during the war."

Shiloh nodded that he could indeed understand her husband's feelings.

"I think his resolve to move west was strengthened because of the destruction he was ordered to carry out during that last campaign through the Shenandoah Valley. He was ashamed of what circumstance required him to do, but he was wise enough to know that in another war it could be *his* family's wealth that was destroyed. So, while the house he built was a direct result of his desire to acknowledge in a visible way his sorrow for the duties he had fulfilled and the move west was necessitated by his growing need for space and distance from the crowded cities, his choice of cattle raising over farming was a simple matter of personal preference and what the land his Uncle Ed chose would support. We grow a vegetable garden to supply the kitchen; we planted an orchard that will on occasion yield fresh fruit, if we can protect the trees from late frost in the spring.

"The house was built in New York, dismantled, marked for reassembly and shipped by rail and wagon to be erected on the ranch, and it is not really suited to the bitter winters we experience here. Something more similar to the log structures I grew up in would have been more practical, but Jonathan lacked the experience to know that, and we only realized it in hindsight."

"You have remained here the two years since your husband's death. Have you any plans to return to the east at some point in the future?"

"No, my daughter was born shortly after we arrived," she said. "We have lived on this ranch almost eleven years; this is our home, and we love it here."

"Was Jonathan a good husband and a good father?" Shiloh asked.

"He loved me and he loved our daughter; he provided well for us and was considerate of our feelings and our needs. He was by no means perfect, but he was a Christian gentleman who worked toward the goal of eternal perfection," she said. "Yes, I think he was a good husband and a good father." She paused for a moment then gently asked. "Was your wife a good wife and a good mother?"

"In the beginning, she was a wonderful mother," Shiloh told her. "And she was probably a better wife than I was a husband. I had known Lydia literally her entire life; she lived on a neighboring plantation. We played together as small children; our mothers were close friends and took turns visiting with each other for several days at a time. I think they planned for us to marry from the time that Lydia was born. When I came home from school at Christmas and for the summers, we spent much time together. We spent many happy days riding together as adolescents. We loved each other, but we were still young when we married. We had never talked about the things that we found were important to us after we married. We really did not know each other.

"I was the typical son of a plantation owner, or we thought I was. I had been raised for a privileged life. A southern gentleman did not labor in the fields; he concerned himself with intellectual and artistic pursuits. I read widely and learned to play the piano. A southern gentleman did not fight with his hands; he learned the use of swords, sabers, dueling pistols, rifles and shotguns for hunting, for self-defense and for war. Oh, a good many of us learned to box, I did at the academy, but that was for sport. I was sent to a military preparatory academy in anticipation of an appointment to West Point; had my father not died at an early age, I would have been expected to spend some years in a military career then become involved in politics prior to taking over the plantation.

"I was taught to hide my emotions; a man, gentleman or otherwise, did not cry. I was to be stoic, impassive, tough. I was never taught how to be affectionate and loving to my wife or son. If my father and mother had any affection for one another, they never displayed it in my presence and certainly never in public. The only example I had of love and affection was from Penny, and her influence ended when I was nine.

"I did not truly understand my own needs, and I certainly had no understanding of Lydia's needs. I loved her, but I knew neither how to tell her nor how to show her. Nor did she understand me. When our son was born, she insisted that he be named after me; rather than call him junior, I continued to be addressed as Paul, and we called him Daniel. And she was a wonderful mother those early years, foregoing the use of a nanny and taking the full responsibility of Daniel's care. Oh, she had servants to do the laundry and prepare meals once he was old enough to eat solid food, but she cared for him, played with him, taught him and loved him. And I loved her for it, and I tried to follow her example, to learn from her.

"But we had our differences from the very beginning. I had already begun to free my slaves when we married, and she neither understood nor agreed. She was afraid that freeing the slaves would cause our social and financial ruin; either would have been a disaster to her. And though my father was not given to considering the feelings of his slaves, as evidenced by selling them with no thought to family connections, he did not abuse his slaves, nor did he whip the rebellious ones. He would not buy a slave who bore marks of the lash, regarding that as an indication of rebellion, so he was shrewd enough not to put marks on his own slaves. His punishment for the first incident of rebellion was to lock the slave into an outdoor jail, a cage, really, and restrict food and water for whatever length of time he determined to be adequate. Unless he was convinced that he would have no second incident of rebellion, he immediately sold that slave.

"And, while I considered my father's way harsh and put an end to such actions soon after his death, Lydia's father ran his plantation in a much more severe fashion. Punishment was commonplace for the smallest infraction. His female slaves were treated as brood mares for the purpose of increasing the numbers and improving the bloodlines of his slave population. While I never heard of him using them as personal concubines as some did, he did subject them to the attentions of male slaves that he used as he would stallions, with no thought to feelings or emotions. And he collected fees from a very small number of other slaveholders for the use of those males in the same way a breeder charges fees for a champion stallion.

"Lydia had been taught and truly believed that negroes were animal rather than human. She would have whipped one as she would have whipped an unruly horse or might have kicked one as she would have kicked a dog that was too slow in getting out of her way, something we never did to slaves, horses or dogs. So we fought from the very beginning over the treatment of the slaves.

"As Daniel grew older, we began to fight over his upbringing. While Lydia still doted over him and treated him with affection, she believed I should be as strict and severe with him as her father had been with her brothers. In her view, it was a mother's prerogative to be affectionate and even permissive, but a father had to be a stern and unyielding example of strength to assure that his sons would become strong and courageous men. And she did not want her son to be taught to regard negroes as I had grown to regard them. While we had both grown up hearing the scriptures taught, I know that I was not truly a Christian at that point in my life, and I don't believe Lydia was either. While ministers in other parts of the south may have distorted scriptures to support slavery and subdue the slaves, in Virginia, they were generally silent on the subject, neither approving nor disapproving, and pointing to Jesus as their example. I suppose it is possible that Lydia could have been a genuine believer and still held to the erroneous beliefs she did regarding the slaves. But I had been convicted in my spirit that slavery was wrong, and I was growing toward the realization that salvation is for all men, free or slave. I was still years away from a true understanding of what all of that meant, but I already knew that what I had been taught was wrong, and I didn't want it taught to my son. So Lydia and I began to fight over that as well."

Shiloh leaned forward, resting his elbows on his knees and cupped his chin in his hands.

"Then I went off to war, never far from the plantation, yet seldom able to return. I don't know if Lydia ever learned to appreciate those former slaves who continued to work the land and provide both food and limited monetary income to her support. We were terribly unhappy with one another at the beginning of the war. I think we both knew that the south could not win a protracted war against the north, so as the years of war dragged on, we both knew that the issue of slavery would be taken out of our hands. But changing laws do not necessarily change attitudes, so I did not know if we could reconcile our differences to the point of becoming friends again. I only knew that I could not yield where Daniel's teaching was concerned; he would have to be taught to live in the world that was going to be his after the war, and I had to convince Lydia of that.

"Then they were murdered, and I had nothing. Well, I had some gold and silver coin hidden away, but I felt dead emotionally. I deeded the remaining land to the servants before it could be stolen by carpetbaggers, and I boarded a ship bound for Europe. I was already trying to drown myself in a whiskey bottle before the ship docked. But I managed for several years to function reasonably well in spite of increased drinking.

"I was adept at playacting; my entire life had truly been playacting to that point, so I managed to preserve the gentlemanly manner to which I had been born and concealed my increasing drunkenness. I had only one useful skill, so I began to give piano lessons to the children of wealthy patrons. I wrote a few musical compositions that came to the attention of some well-respected musicians and conductors. When I demonstrated an unusual talent in performing on the piano, I was invited to work with those musicians and conductors. Later, when a few of the more well-known pianists had to turn down an offer to perform, for whatever reason, they began to recommend me as a replacement, and soon I was touring from city to city for piano concerts.

"But I continued to drink more and more, and I grew less and less able to conceal my drunkenness. My performances at the piano suffered, and I grew bitter and belligerent. I was thrown into the local version of the 'drunk tank' several times in several different countries. In London, I was arrested and facing charges that could have sent me to prison. I was released thanks to the influence of an Earl who had heard me perform, an Earl whose father had lost the family fortune through poor management, so that the Earl had only his title, his land, his political responsibilities as a member of the House of Lords and his personal responsibilities to employees who were the descendents of those who had once been serfs on the estate. The Earl had learned to work right alongside them, and he had become a devout and compassionate Christian along the way. He had also fought his own battle against alcohol, so he knew what it took to win. He met me where I was, as Jesus had met so many during His life on this earth, and he showed me how Jesus, through the work of the Holy Spirit is still meeting us where we are."

Sarah laid her right hand on Shiloh's left shoulder, and he turned toward her, smiling.

"After a few years, I was ready to stand once more on my own two feet. I had learned some measure of humility and a great deal about being loved. It was time for me to leave, but I had no idea where God wanted me to go. I boarded a boat bound for Galveston, Texas. Once there, I worked at an assortment of jobs and eventually became skilled at handling cattle. When I felt led to move on, I signed on with a trail herd headed to Kansas. Once there, I felt directed toward Montana Territory. I can't explain exactly how or why that happens, but I believe God is pointing me toward His purpose. I think it is His purpose at this time for me to help you find out who has been shooting your hands. I have tried to learn to be content to complete one purpose before worrying about where He will send me next. For a man who has been placed in authority over other men for much of his life, learning to follow, to serve, is not easy."

"It may not be easy for you," Sarah said. "But you seem to have become very skilled at serving others. You have certainly done far more here than is required of a working cowboy. And I thank you sincerely for the risks you are taking to help us."

"I just wish I knew why someone is so determined to force you to leave. If I knew why, I think I could figure out who," Shiloh told her. "Do you still keep in touch with Clara and the Hadleys? If a railroad is to be built or something else of significant financial profit is being planned for this area, your father-in-law or his associates may well have some idea of what that something is.

Perhaps a telegram to him would help us to gain useful information."

"Clara and I exchange letters regularly, and I write to Grace, Jonathan's mother, several times a year, mostly to keep her up to date on Hannah's growth." Sarah told him. "But I have not written directly to Mr. Hadley, and I have not met Clara's husband, James Bancroft, although, I do know that he is involved in the running of his family's railroad interests, so he may actually be better informed of plans to build a railroad than Thomas Hadley. It would not be inappropriate for me to inquire by telegram to either. If you will help me compose the questions, I shall be happy to write them out and have you send them in my name. But I think the nearest telegraph office is in Helena, so you would have a long ride and might have to wait several days for the answers."

"Then I should probably pack some supplies and continue on toward Helena after I've met with Michael O'Brien." Shiloh paused for a moment. "Mrs. Hadley, if I should be delayed, or if you and Caleb need help while I'm gone, O'Brien is a trustworthy man and has offered to come to work for you. Believing he may be able to learn more while continuing to work for the Slash V, I've asked him to wait. But I've told Caleb, and I want you to know that you can go to him for help."

"If the need arises, I shall." Sarah assured him. "And, when the time is right, we will certainly be able to put him to work on the ranch. Caleb shares your opinion of his worth, and I have learned to trust both of you in judging men."

CHAPTER ELEVEN

Shiloh had been waiting in the small canyon a bit more than an hour when Michael O'Brien rode in leading a pair of horses with empty packsaddles. Shiloh handed O'Brien a cup of coffee as soon as his boots touched the ground.

"No Irish whiskey," Shiloh apologized and took the reins from O'Brien's hand. "I'll tie your horses with mine."

"Thanks," O'Brien said and tasted the coffee. "General, sir, during the war, did anyone ever tell you that the main reason we kept you around camp was because you made such good coffee?"

"Even when we didn't have real coffee?"

"Especially when we didn't have real coffee," the Irishman said with a large grin. "Lad, good coffee sure warms a man's innards on a day like this when you can feel the coming of winter in the air."

"And a good fire warms the outside," Shiloh said as he placed a couple of sticks carefully into the blaze.

"You best be careful, or you'll have me wishing we were back in the war."

"Not likely," Shiloh said. "But what have you been doing with yourself in the years since? How did you end up in the west?"

"Well, after the war, there was no law in the south, except for

Union troops, and they were afraid in the beginning that some of us old soldiers would form partisan groups and continue to fight a guerilla war, so they wisely kept together for defensive strength. That left most of the south unprotected, especially where the southern soldiers hadn't reached home yet, and there was a lot of riffraff doing a lot of mischief—ex-soldiers from the north and the south, freed slaves—didn't matter where they were from or what color their skin, they were a bad bunch doing a lot of meanness. So some of us got permission from the Union commanders to form local military police units to protect the countryside. We'd catch the renegades; the Union army would punish them. I led one such group in our county until the establishment of a military post at the county seat eliminated the need for our unit."

"I never anticipated that problem," Shiloh admitted. "Maybe if I'd stayed to help restore order, I could have made a difference."

"Maybe so, but you had your own troubles to deal with."

"I did, and it took a few years," Shiloh said. "But maybe if I'd had some more important purpose I could have avoided the mistakes. Oh, well, water under the bridge. What brought you west?"

"When law and order returned to the south, I went to work for the railroad, laying new tracks or repairing old ones. After about five years of doing that, I ended up in Dodge. Met a couple of buffalo runners who offered to teach me the trade, so I spent most of '71 on the plains with them. Then I bought my own outfit, hired some skinners and went into business for myself."

"You were a buffalo hunter?"

"Buffalo *runner*," O'Brien corrected. "Although, the only time we actually ran buffalo was when we wanted to show off. The Indians ran them on horseback, mostly with lances, stabbing them behind the ribs over and over until they'd carve up something vital or the buffalo lost enough blood to go down. Running buffalo was exciting, but dangerous if your horse stepped in a prairie dog hole, of which there were plenty, and it wasn't profitable, so we hunted from a stand. But anyone who called himself a buffalo hunter was a tenderfoot for sure. We called ourselves buffalo runners."

"What made you want to go after buffalo?"

"Partly for the adventure," O'Brien admitted. "But mostly it was the lure of money—it was like a gold rush. I once heard there were twenty thousand men chasing after twenty million buffalo. Both numbers are likely double what the real figures were, but at two or three dollars a hide and storebought cartridges costing no more that twenty-five cents, I figured to kill a hundred buffalo a day and make four to six thousand dollars a month after expenses—a hundred times the average working man's wage."

"Did you?" Shiloh asked.

"The first year, '71, I went out with a Scotsman named Ian Stewart and a German named Charles Schmidt. I didn't even own a proper rifle. I'd bought a 'yellowboy' Winchester shortly after the war, and I used it to hunt camp meat and drive off troublesome Indians, but it wasn't suitable for buffalo running. So I'd borrow a rifle from either Ian or Charlie, depending on who I went with on a particular day. At the end of the trip, they cut me in for a full share, and they knew the business so that was a tidy sum. I took that and a couple of thousand dollars I'd managed not to spend on Irish whiskey while laying railroad tracks and bought my own outfit.

"Choosing a rifle was the hardest decision I had to make, and there were really only two choices at the time, a Sharps or a Remington. Either was accurate and powerful enough for a dropping kill—that's what we called it when one bullet brought the buffalo down.

"Stewart was a Remington man—Schmidt, a Sharps man, so I had a chance to try both, and I listened closely when the two argued over which was better. I finally chose to go with the Sharps because I think the action is stronger, the Sharps has a big side hammer than can be cocked wearing mittens on the coldest day of winter, and the straight cartridge seemed less likely than the bottleneck Remington casing to become distorted after being fired and reloaded over and over. And reloading cost about half what a new factory cartridge did, so I reloaded.

"Charlie had a matched pair of 40-90 models with double-set triggers and 20-power full-length one-inch tube telescopes on the 32-inch barrels. I talked him into selling me one, after he talked me out of the mistake of buying a 45-70."

O'Brien grinned at Shiloh and winked.

"You might be surprised to know that the government, through the army, supplies the buffalo runners with free ammunition."

"Why?" Shiloh asked.

"When Sheridan was put in command of the western troops, he proposed to bring peace by wiping out the buffalo that support the Indians' way of life. 'Kill the buffalo,' he said. 'And you kill the Indians.' I guess he figures that without the buffalo, the Indians will be less independent and more willing to move onto the reservations. Charlie Schmidt told me Sheridan believed it was a matter of killing either the Indians or the buffalo, and that killing the buffalo was more humane."

"Makes sense, I guess," Shiloh admitted reluctantly. "The ranchers won't mind seeing the buffalo gone, more grass for the cattle. And the army gave you free ammunition?"

"I got thousands of rounds of army issue 45-70 caliber, and my first thought was to buy a rifle chambered for it." O'Brien told him. "Instead, I pulled the bullets, melted the lead to mold into the 320 grain bullets for the 40-90 and used the government lead and powder. Then Charlie found some excellent English powders and wouldn't use anything else, so I followed his lead and never had reason to regret it, even though it cost half again as much as American powder. We were able to use 420 grain bullets with the English powder, and we traded the government powder."

"Those cartridges in your belt look bigger than 40-90."

"They're 45-110-550 cartridges," O'Brien told him. "When Christian Sharps introduced his 'Sharps Old Reliable' rifle, I had to have one. Cost me twice what I paid Charlie for the 40-90-320, and there is very little difference in accuracy, range or power. But it's the biggest and the best of the Sharps buffalo rifles."

"What'd you do with the 40-90?"

"Kept it until I ran into Charlie; he insisted on buying it back."

"You were going to tell me about all the money to be made," Shiloh reminded.

"Don't be impatient, laddie; I'm coming to that." O'Brien said. "I didn't shoot a hundred buffalo a day like I'd planned on. On an average day, I shot twenty-five. If the skinners were well-rested, I might shoot twice that many. Shooting more than the skinners could handle was a waste of expensive cartridges. The first two years there were plenty of buffalo, and I did fairly well; my share of the net was around $2,500.00. The third year, '74, was my best year at just under $3,000.00. By '75, the buff were getting hard to find, and I got out of the business. Stewart and Schmidt did as well or better than I did every year, and they're still running buffalo as far as I know. But few did as well as we did; the average runner probably made less than $1,000.00 a year. Nobody made the four to six thousand dollars a month I went in dreaming about, and nobody will—the buff are about gone."

"Do you regret it?" Shiloh asked.

"I'm still making up my mind about that," O'Brien admitted. "I had to make a living, and there were millions of buffalo. It never occurred to me that we could kill them all. If Sheridan is right about the choice being between killing the Indian or the buffalo, then maybe, by helping to destroy his way of life, I helped to save his life. But I had to shoot a few Indians to save my own life.

"As for the adventure part, once I had the right rifle and had acquired the necessary skill, shooting buffalo was about as adventurous as shooting cattle in a corral. Running buffalo was a lot like the war, days of waiting for a few minutes of excitement, and the excitement often involved stampeding buffalo or Indian attacks, adventures you were glad you'd gone through, some that you never wanted to go through again."

"I guess I should tell you that when you get back to the Slash V you're going to find out that you're talking to a ghost," Shiloh told him. "Caleb rode into White Sulphur Springs this morning to tell the town marshal that I was shot by our unknown sharpshooter day before yesterday." Shiloh told him the whole story. "Reverend Reardon will likely have my funeral in a few days, and I'll have my feelings badly hurt if you don't show up."

"With the preacher there, Mrs. Hadley probably won't serve any Irish whiskey to drown my sorrow."

"Probably wouldn't even if he wasn't there."

"If I go to this funeral, are you going to expect me to go to your next one?"

"I promised Caleb I'd try to keep him from having to dig another grave, it being such an added burden to go with his other chores. Maybe, if I can manage to live forever, I won't bring any more grief to either of you."

"Laddie, if you can manage to live forever, I'd be pleased to throw in with you."

"Well, I've already learned the secret to eternal life," Shiloh said. "And the Bible says that not all of us will die, that some will be changed 'in the twinkling of an eye from mortal to immortal.'"

"The Bible say when that's going to happen?" O'Brien asked.

"Maybe. I don't know yet."

"And you've learned the secret to eternal life?"

"Actually, it's not a secret, and I grew up thinking I already knew what it meant, but I didn't. I had to find the bottom of my last bottle of whiskey before I was ready for God to introduce me to a man who could introduce me to Him."

"Are you telling me I have to give up Irish whiskey before I can meet God?"

"No, *I* had to because I was too drunk and too angry and too proud to ask for God's help. Eternal life is a free gift. I didn't deserve it, and I couldn't earn it. Once I came to that understanding, accepting the gift became a lot easier."

"Laddie, you've lost me," O'Brien told him. "I don't have a clue as to what you're talking about. I guess the little boy me sainted mother dragged to mass should have learned Latin and listened to the priest."

"Might not have done you any good. I thought I was listening to the preaching in English, and I missed the whole meaning of the mystery."

"Well, maybe you should tell me the meaning of the mystery."

"I'll try. It started with Adam and Eve in the Garden of Eden. When they ate fruit from the forbidden tree, their disobedience caused their immediate spiritual death and later physical death; they were created to live forever. God called their disobedience sin, and we all inherited that sin from Adam and Eve. No matter how good or honorable we may be or try to become, not one of us is or can be perfect, but eternal life in God's presence demands perfection. So God provided a way for us to be made perfect; He sent His Son Jesus to die in our place, a perfect and sinless substitute to accept the punishment for our failure to be perfect and sinless. If we believe that Jesus is the Son of God and the Savior He said He was, if we accept that we are not perfect and ask to be made perfect, God, through Jesus, will make us perfect and restore to us the eternal life that was our intended inheritance."

"And you've done that and are now perfect?" O'Brien asked.

Shiloh grinned at his friend.

"That's really the mystery part," he said. "No, I'm not perfect, not yet. At some point, after physical death or when we are changed 'in the twinkling of an eye' I will be made perfect. But, because I have accepted God's gift of salvation, He sees me as perfect even now and has forgiven me for sins past, present and future. So, even though I can still die or be killed in this mortal body, I have His promise of eternal life in an immortal body."

"And you expect me to believe all that?"

"*God* expects you to believe all that," Shiloh corrected. "He calls it faith, and, if you ask Him, He will provide even the faith to believe in His Son and in His plan for salvation."

"Sounds too simple, too easy," O'Brien said.

"It did to me, too," Shiloh admitted. "I wanted to work for it, to earn it—to *deserve* salvation. But Jesus did all that for me, and for you. Eternal life is a gift. God won't take it back. I may be able to throw it away; there's some disagreement, and I'm not sure where I stand on that issue just yet."

"I guess I need to think on the whole subject some."

"We can talk again another time," Shiloh said. "And if that sharpshooter manages to kill me before I can stop him, you can talk to Reverend Pearson or anybody on the J H Connected."

"Even the little girl?" O'Brien asked.

"Even the little girl," Shiloh said. "Maybe, *especially* Hannah; children seem to have an easier time understanding and accepting God's Word than adults do. Probably because God says we have to approach Him as a little child, and that's a hard thing for proud men to do."

"Well, how can I help you stop the sharpshooter before he gets another shot at you?"

"I don't know," Shiloh said. "I was hoping you might have heard or seen something that would help. Tell me about Frank Vickers and his son George."

"Frank is a hard man, but an honest one. I don't trust George, and I don't much like him, but he's not your sharpshooter."

"You're sure?"

"I've seen him shoot," O'Brien said. "Up close, he's fairly good with a handgun, but he can't hit anything with a rifle beyond a hundred yards or so. No way could he hit three men with three bullets at distances from three hundred yards out to eight hundred."

"Who could?"

"I could with my Sharps," O'Brien said. "Most any of the buffalo runners could at distances out to six hundred yards, and a good many could probably shoot accurately to seven or eight hundred. Either of the two men who taught me could do it."

"Doesn't narrow it down much, does it? Why don't you trust George Vickers?"

"I don't know, exactly—call it instinct. The only thing I can say for sure is that he's hired a dozen new men we didn't need to work cattle, men who seem to be better with guns than ropes. I haven't heard any plans or plots or conspiracies, mostly because anytime I get near a group of them talking, they shut up."

"Have you ever heard George talk about Sarah Hadley? Hannah thinks he plans to marry her, and Caleb worries about the way he looks at her."

"I'd say Hannah is right; can't say as I blame him—she's a beautiful woman and a real lady."

"She is that," Shiloh agreed.

"I haven't heard George say anything about the lady, but I did once hear him mention her ranch as if it were going to be a part of the Slash V. And, while he isn't the shooter, I wouldn't put it past him to hire a rifleman to shoot all her hands."

"Do you think Frank Vickers could be a part of any such plans?"

"I don't think so, and with his wife long dead, I think George is his one soft spot. If George is behind some plan to marry Sarah Hadley and take over the J H Connected, I don't think Frank could be made to see it very easily. The odd part is why George would think he needed to kill off all her hands. I guess he's what a woman would consider a handsome man, and she's lost her husband. As arrogant as George is, why wouldn't he think he could just win her affections through courtship?"

"I don't know," Shiloh admitted. "Do you think George could have had anything to do with Jonathan Hadley's death? Caleb has doubts as to that being an accident."

"Honestly, I wouldn't put anything past George Vickers, but I don't have a shred of evidence to suggest any wrongdoing on his part."

"Well, keep your eyes and ears open. I'm going to ride on to

Helena and send a few telegrams to see if I can learn what may be behind the shootings."

"One of the men who was in my military police detachment is a Pinkerton agent now. Name's Brent Madison; send him a telegram in my name."

"Thanks, I will. And if you get a chance, you might look in on things at the J H Connected while I'm gone."

CHAPTER TWELVE

Shiloh rode west several hours after leaving O'Brien before making camp for the night. He spent the second night in a mining camp on the east side of the Big Belt Mountains, hoping to learn something of significance from the miners. Learning little, he was in the saddle at first light, rode west over Duck Creek Pass, then northwest to the Missouri River. He bought a few supplies in J. V. Stafford's general store then crossed the river before nightfall on the canyon ferry Stafford had bought from John Oakes ten years earlier. Once safely across the river, he camped for the night before riding the remaining ten miles into Helena on the fourth day.

Shiloh found a livery barn for his horse, made arrangements to sleep in the hayloft for a few nights and was directed to the telegraph office by the hostler. He sent telegrams to Thomas Hadley, James Bancroft and Brent Madison, ate his noon meal in the boarding house where the telegrapher lived and had recommended the fare. Then he spent the afternoon walking about Helena, visiting several saloons and stores, listening to the topics of conversation while asking very few questions. He stopped by the telegraph office just before it closed for the evening and picked up telegrams acknowledging receipt of his queries and promising answers as soon as the information could be obtained. Then Shiloh settled in to wait.

* * * * * * *

On the morning Shiloh left for Helena, Caleb rode into White Sulphur Springs to report the shooting.

"That sharpshooter's been out to the J H Connected ag'in, Marshal," he said to Dan Hobbs as he stepped through the door to his office.

The wizened old marshal removed wire-framed glasses from his pale blue eyes and pushed aside the stack of papers he was reading, then he stood up and walked from behind his desk to shake Caleb's hand. The morning sun streaming through the front windows of his office added red highlights to light brown hair that flowed into short, white sideburns.

"Who is it this time—that new man, Shiloh, who was in church with the Hadleys last Sunday?" he asked.

"Yep."

"I'm sorry to hear that; he looked like a solid citizen. I was hoping he might help you catch that bushwhacker."

"You heard anythin' about when the territorial marshal might get out this way to look into things?" Caleb asked.

"Nope," Hobbs said. "But I'll send him another letter reporting this new shooting and maybe add a prod about asking the governor of the territory to send a special investigator."

"That'll likely make him mad at you."

"Yeah, but since he's appointed by the governor, it might get him out of his chair and into his saddle," Hobbs said with a wry grin. "If it don't, I'll just have to send a letter to the governor saying how all the folks in my town are scared to death about this killer, afraid to leave town for fear of their lives—maybe talk about citizens sending letters to the president and even to the big city newspapers back east."

"Any of that actually happenin'?" Caleb asked.

"Well," the town marshal said with a wink, "I don't know that it is exactly, but I don't know that it ain't either."

"Yore a sly ol' fox, Dan," Caleb said. "But I wouldn't want folks to think you'd lie. I cain't read nor write. Shiloh was teaching me. But I can ask the preacher to write a letter or two along them lines fer me, maybe get him to write some fer hisself or suggest that ever'body in the church start doin' it."

"You do that, Caleb," Hobbs told him. "And I'll mention it to the territorial marshal. Might be, though, that those letters ought to go to the governor first before we start appealing to the president."

"I've only met the governor one time, when I rode in to Helena with the Colonel several years back," Caleb said. "But I can just see that pompous windbag sputterin' threats at the territorial marshal if he don't do somethin' to settle folks down."

"Well," Hobbs said. "That's politics and politicians."

"Never cared much fer neither," Caleb told him.

"That's mostly why I decided to come west to be marshal of a sleepy little cowtown."

Caleb poked him in the ribs with a bony finger.

"An' I thought it was 'cause you'd got old an' lazy."

"Well, I ain't as old as you," Hobbs said then grinned widely and added. "But I'll try to make up for it in lazy."

"You ought not to have no problems there," Caleb said agreeably. "Reckon I better go see the preacher about readin' over the new grave I dug."

* * * * * * *

The preacher was sitting in the parsonage porch swing reading his Bible when Caleb rode up.

"Working on my sermon for Sunday," he said as Caleb eased out of his saddle. "What brings you to town in the middle of the week?" he asked as he met Caleb at the top of the porch steps.

"Need to have you read some words over a new grave I helped

dig yesterday."

Something in Caleb's words and manner led Reardon to wonder.

"Is there somebody in that grave?"

"Nope," Caleb told him. "But we want folks to think there is. I didn't exactly lie to Dan Hobbs, but I shore didn't straighten him out when he come to the conclusions I meant fer him to."

"Who's supposed to be dead? Shiloh?"

"Yep," Caleb told him. "This time that sneakin' sharpshooter missed, but we don't want him to know it. As long as he thinks Shiloh's dead, he won't come huntin' him ag'in, and' it might give us a chance to catch him before he shoots somebody else."

"I'm not sure but what I don't wish you'd let me think he was dead, too," Reardon said ruefully. "Would have hurt to think he'd been killed, I really do like Shiloh, but I don't know how I'm going to give a eulogy for a man who isn't dead." He shook his head at Caleb. "Oh, well, if it'll help prevent another death, I'm sure the Lord will show me. Do you want us to come out to the ranch tomorrow afternoon?"

"That'd be real nice," Caleb said. "I'll spread the word around town before I head back to the ranch. And you could do me another favor that might help."

The two men talked about the letters Dan Hobbs had suggested, and Reardon agreed to write letters for both Caleb and himself and to encourage the townspeople to write letters as well. He also told Caleb that he should suggest that Sarah Hadley write letters of her own, since the J H Connected was the ranch at risk.

On the way back through town, Caleb stopped in at Jenkins' store and saloon to spread the word about the funeral the next afternoon, and he stopped again at the marshal's office to tell him personally and to let him know what the preacher had agreed to about writing the letters. Then he rode back to the J H Connected.

* * * * * * *

The next morning after breakfast, Caleb took a scythe and began cutting hay in a meadow a couple of miles from the ranch house. He worked alone until noon, praying as he worked, asking God's forgiveness if his part of the funeral deception was a sin, and seeking guidance in the search for the sharpshooter. He prayed for Shiloh's safety and for the safety of the Hadleys. Finally, he prayed that God would keep him strong enough to serve some useful purpose on the ranch.

Caleb worked through the morning, pacing himself so that he made steady progress without wearing himself down too quickly between rest breaks. As the position of the sun told him it was nearing midday, he visually surveyed the several acres he had cut and was satisfied that he hadn't wasted the morning. He mounted his horse and was almost to the house when he heard Hannah clanging the triangle to let him know it was time for the noon meal.

"Caleb," Hannah said, as he washed his hands and face on the back porch. "Mother and I are going to start helping you with the haying. You can teach us to use a scythe."

"Well, I've no doubt both of you could learn, an' yore gettin' to be a purty grown up girl these days, but it's mighty hard work, an' the scythe would shore leave cruel blisters on yore hands. Maybe we could start the two of you out rakin' the hay while I load it in the wagon with a pitchfork." He dried his face and hands then hung the towel back on its peg. "I'd shore hate fer you to hurt yore hands so bad you couldn't play the piano fer me. An' you an' yore momma do a heap of work with cookin' an' gardenin', feedin' the chickens an' gatherin' the eggs. Don't go to feelin' yore not doin' yore share."

"But it's too much work for just you, even with Shiloh to help, and he won't be back for at least a week," Hannah argued.

"I'll be grateful fer yore help," Caleb said sincerely. "But I want yore promise that you'll start slow an' careful, pay attention to what I tell you an' stop when I say so."

"You know I will!"

"Then let's eat," he said. "We've got some more playactin' to do this afternoon."

* * * * * * *

After the meal, Caleb went down to the bunkhouse to get his suitcoat, while Sarah and Hannah changed into Sunday dresses. Then he and Sarah settled in to wait on the porch while Hannah practiced at the piano.

Frank and George Vickers and Michael O'Brien were the first to arrive. George went straight to Sarah.

"I told that fool he'd get himself shot if he didn't clear out, but he was too bull-headed to listen," George told her. "Anyway, we came across a bunch of your cows pretty far north and drove them south as we came, so they'd be closer to the ranch for the winter."

"It was O'Brien's idea," Frank Vickers told her. "Should have thought of it myself." He did not see the annoyed look the admission evoked from his son. His wide smile was warm, but his resemblance to his son was unquestionable, with the same brown eyes and hair. He was a brawny, heavy man with powerful muscles and a square jaw marred by a puckered scar from the hoof of a steer that objected to being branded. "We noticed a meadow a few miles back with some fresh cut hay. O'Brien is handy with a scythe, and George hired enough extra men this summer that I could loan O'Brien to you until you get your hay in for the winter."

"That is very kind of you, Mr. Vickers," Sarah told him. "I know Caleb will appreciate the help."

"Then it's settled." He turned to O'Brien. "You might as well stay here and go to work after the funeral. I'll send one of the hands over with your bedroll and anything else you need out of your kitbag."

"The Swede sleeps in the bunk above mine," O'Brien told him. "He knows my stuff from his; might as well send it all; otherwise, I might need something I didn't remember to ask for."

"Caleb, you got an extra blanket or two O'Brien can use tonight if I wait 'til morning to send the Swede over with his bedroll and kitbag?" Frank asked.

"I'm shore I can find him somethin'," Caleb said. "Come on, O'Brien, let's go down to the bunkhouse an' have a look." Caleb turned to go, then turned back. "Mr. Vickers, might be a good idea not to let it be knowed that you've loaned us O'Brien. Fewer folks that know, less likely he is to be the next one shot."

"I agree," Frank told him. "I'll make sure my hands know not to be loose-lipped."

With that, Caleb led O'Brien toward the bunkhouse. He waited until they were far enough away not to be heard before saying anything else.

"What'd you have to do to persuade Frank to let you help us?"

"It was his idea," O'Brien said. "On the way over here, he decided it was time he quit minding his own business and started helping a neighbor in need. Said he was going to send a rider out to the other ranches and ask for the loan of the best hunters and trackers in the country to go after this killer."

"How'd George react to that?" Caleb asked as they went through the bunkhouse door.

"Didn't like it at all," O'Brien told him. "Argued that it'd likely just get some of their own people killed."

"You think George is really worried about the Slash V hands?"

"Unless George actually hired this sharpshooter for some plan of his own that he doesn't want ruined, I'd say the only thing George is worried about is not becoming one of the killer's victims."

"What do you think of Frank's plan?" Caleb asked.

"Well, Frank might get lucky, but, unless this killer is working ahead of some close deadline, I'd say a hunting party would likely only cause him to sit tight and wait until they get tired of looking for him before he shoots anyone else. That's what I'd do, if I was him."

"Me, too," Caleb agreed. "Take any bunk you want. Nights are getting colder, so you might want one close to that pot-bellied stove. Blankets on all the bunks; if you need extry take as many as you like. Miz Hadley washed 'em all after the last of the hands run out on her. Been no complaints about bedbugs, lice or the like, so if they start bein' a problem, I'll blame you fer bringin' 'em."

"Thanks." O'Brien said sarcastically.

He was about to say more when they heard the sounds of wagons and buggies.

"Reckon that'll be the preacher an' the folks from town," Caleb said.

The cavalcade was only one buggy, the Reardons, and one wagon driven by Smoke, the bartender, and carrying Jenkins, the storekeeper. Dan Hobbs was riding horseback alongside the Reardons' buggy.

"Smoke, would you see that the team gets some water?" Jenkins gave the order as a request while he climbed down from the seat.

"Sho', Boss, Ah'll see to 'em."

Caleb climbed up beside him.

"Thanks for coming, Smoke; I'll show you where to take the team."

"Marshal," O'Brien said. "Tie your horse to the preacher's buggy, and I'll take him to water along with theirs." O'Brien held the Reardons' horse still as the preacher climbed down and helped his wife to the ground.

"Thank you, Michael," Reardon said. "No need to hurry. I'll wait a little while before I begin in case someone else is coming."

"Yes, sir," O'Brien acknowledged as he climbed into the buggy seat and started after the wagon.

As the wagon was approaching a shady spot at the edge of the beaver pond, Caleb asked Smoke why he always came to the funerals on the ranch.

"'Cuz they wuz men Ah knew," he said. "An' eveh one of 'em treated me wif respect."

"Did you know Shiloh?"

"Seen him in the saloon last Saturday; he bought a couple of drinks fo' Mr. O'Brien an' asked very politely fo' a mug of cool water fo' hisself." Smoke hesitated then looked carefully at Caleb before continuing. "Mebbe Ah ought not to say, since he wuz usin' anutha name, but Ah don' see what it ken hurt now that he's daid. Ah knowed him befo', when Ah wuz a boy. Befo' the war he owned a plantation; he owned mah daddy an' mah sister. Mah momma wuz his mammy befo' his momma sold her. One evenin' he showed up on the plantation wheah Ah wuz born, bought Momma an' me an' took us home to be wif Daddy an' Daisy. Then he set us free, not just us, but all uh his slaves. Ah neveh had no mo' use fo' his wife than she did fo' me, but Ah liked his boy. It wuz mah job to see he didn' git hurt or into no trouble on the plantation. Ah taught him to fish an' to git along in the woods. Dan'l would've been as good a man as his daddy, if'n he hadn' been murdered by yankee deserters. An' Massuh Clifton wuz the finest man Ah eveh knowed."

Caleb stared in amazement as tears streamed down the huge black man's cheeks, then he decided.

"Don't let on, Smoke, but he ain't dead."

Smoke turned in astonishment.

"Is you tellin' me the gospel truth?"

"Yep, that sharpshooter finally missed."

"Praise the Lord an' hallelujah!"

O'Brien pulled up beside them in time to hear Smoke's outburst.

"You two holding a revival meeting?"

"I just told him the man who gave him his freedom is still alive," Caleb said.

O'Brien took a close look at Smoke and smiled in wonder.

"Only other man I ever knew as big as you was Jimbo, an' you

125

do look like him. Are you Tommy?"

"Heah Ah is," Smoke grinned.

O'Brien stuck out his hand and took Smoke's in a firm grip.

"I saw you once at the start of the war. You were a gangly teenager, long on bone and gristle, short on meat."

"Ah remembers," Smoke said. "It wuz the last time Ah saw Massuh Clifton 'til he bought you them drinks on Saturday. Seemed like eveh time he got to come home durin' the war, I wuz gone on some errand. Wheah is he now, if'n he ain't daid?"

"Tryin' to find out why somebody wants the Hadleys off this ranch," Caleb told him.

"Tell him Ah'd like to see him ag'in when it's safe," Smoke said. "Tell him Ah'll be prayin' fo' him."

"I will, Smoke," Caleb assured him. "An' if you hear anythin' that will help, get word to us."

"Ah will," Smoke promised. "The Hadleys is good people."

O'Brien climbed down to lead the marshal's horse to the edge of the pond.

"Smoke?" Caleb asked. "You told me why you come to the funerals. Why do you suppose Jenkins comes? Must cost him to close the store."

"Oh, he don' close the sto'," Smoke said. "Any time he wants to run errands or get away fo' awhile, one of us runs the sto'. Charlie's tendin' bar today, so Jake is mindin' the sto'. As fo' him comin' to the funerals, he says they wuz all customers, an' it's good business to show folks he cares when one of 'em passes."

"Smoke?" O'Brien asked. "In the last week or two, do you remember seeing a tall man in a black frock coat and wearing a planter's hat?"

"Nah, suh, Ah don'," Smoke told him. "But Ah don' stay in town much when Ah ain't workin' fo' wages—Ah'm usually workin' on mah own place, or fishin' if'n the streams ain't froze."

CHAPTER THIRTEEN

The Reverend Timothy Reardon had spent as much time in prayer about this particular eulogy as he had on any funeral where the subject was truly deceased, for very different reasons.

"The man we knew as Shiloh had been among us for only a few short days when he became the target of a sneaking, skulking sharpshooter who had already taken the lives of three men trying to earn their wages and help a widow and her daughter hold onto their home. I only had one opportunity to spend time with Shiloh, but in those few hours I found him to be a man of unusual humility, a man who had known much sorrow and pain, a man who had found the saving grace of our Savior and had grown strong in his devotion and dedication to live his life as a servant of God.

"Among my fellow clergymen, there is a difference of opinion as to where the souls of the saved go when we pass from this life. Some believe we go to a place of waiting until the final judgment; some think we go directly into the presence of God. Since Jesus told the thief on the cross 'today you will be with me in Paradise,' I believe we will immediately join the Savior. I wish Shiloh was standing here among us today, so that we could all know him better. But this I truly believe; wherever Shiloh is at this very moment, our Lord is there with him."

The Reverend closed with a prayer for Shiloh and for the safety and well-being of the Hadleys, those who tried to help them and for the community at large. He prayed that God would quickly bring the murderer to justice before any more good men were killed. He was unaware that only four of those present did not know Shiloh was alive, and, while he had not uttered a single lie, he felt deceitful for having carried out this charade, so he closed with a silent prayer for God's forgiveness.

"Thank you for coming, Pastor," Sarah said as she walked beside him to the buggy. She stopped to hug his wife, a petite woman with warm brown eyes and streaks of gray in her dark hair. "And thank you, Ann."

As Dan Hobbs approached his horse, Sarah called out to him.

"Marshal, wait a moment, please, I have something for you." She turned to her daughter. "Hannah, would you please bring the letters on your father's desk." As Hannah ran up the steps to get them, Sarah turned back to the marshal. "I have written letters to the territorial marshal and to the governor seeking immediate action to stop this assassin. I thought you might like to read them before they go out, so I have left them unsealed. Would you post them for me, please?"

"I will," Hobbs promised. "And I'll include your requests in my own report."

"Thank you," Sarah said, as Hannah came running out and handed the letters to the marshal.

When the buggy and wagon rolled away, the marshal mounted up to follow. Frank Vickers started for his own horse, but George lingered a moment longer.

"Sarah," he said. "I'll ride this way in a week or two, and we'll talk. I have a plan that will end your worries."

Without waiting for her to reply, he turned and walked swiftly to catch up with his father. As the two rode away, Sarah wondered aloud.

"What plan could he possibly have that would end all my

worries?"

Caleb had an idea he did not voice; the prospect was unthinkable. Instead, he turned to O'Brien.

"You feel like cuttin' some hay?"

"I feel like cutting something," he answered. "Might as well be hay."

"Let me git out of this suitcoat, an' we'll find you a scythe an' a fresh horse; the one you rode over here has prob'ly done enough fer one day. You're a big man."

"Beside most men, I am; I always feel small next to Smoke. Strongest man I've ever seen—handles a full barrel of Irish whiskey like you or I would a bucket of water."

"Miz Hadley, Hannah, remind us at supper to tell you what we found out about Smoke an' Shiloh today," Caleb said.

"We'll do that," Sarah said. "And we'll have supper ready about dark, so you can plan to ride in while there is still some light to see by."

"Don't worry," O'Brien told her. "Shiloh told me yesterday that you and Hannah cook the best food he's ever eaten. I don't aim to let this skinny old mountain man make me late for any meals!"

"We'll do our best to see that you are not disappointed," Hannah teased.

"You do that, young lady!"

As the two men walked off toward the bunkhouse, both were chuckling. Hannah turned immediately serious.

"Mother, I think George Vickers plans to marry you. I know he's rich, and I guess you might think he's handsome, but I don't trust him. He makes up to me when you're around, but he ignores me when you aren't. And he said some mean things to Shiloh on the way to my music lesson Saturday."

"Hannah, you need not worry that I will marry George Vickers. We have money enough that we do not need his. And while he is certainly handsome on the outside, it is what is on the inside that is important. And when you are old enough to begin looking for a husband of your own, remember that we are not to be unequally yoked. I do not believe George is truly a Christian, even though he does sometimes come to church. You want to find a man of good character like your father was and like Caleb is. I do not believe George Vickers is such a man, so I could never marry him."

"Do you think Shiloh is a man of good character?" Hannah asked.

"I believe Shiloh is a man of very good character."

"As good as Father or Caleb?"

"Every bit as good."

"I told Shiloh he should marry you."

"Oh, you did, did you?" Sarah laughed. "And what was his response?"

"He couldn't think of a single reason why you would want to marry 'a broken down old saddle tramp' like him."

"You like him a lot, do you not?"

"I love him, Mother," Hannah said. "As much as I love Caleb, maybe as much as I love you. And he treats me like Father did. I never want to forget Father, and no one will ever take his place, but Shiloh has made his own place in my heart. I wish you would marry him."

"He might not want to marry me," Sarah said honestly.

"Why wouldn't he? You're beautiful, and you're good, and you cook the best food he's ever eaten."

"*We* cook the best food he has ever eaten." Sarah laughed and hugged her daughter. "Do you think we can win Shiloh with your peach pie?"

"I think we can win Shiloh by loving him."

"Maybe you are right, young lady. And I will have to admit that I have strong feelings for him, too. We should both pray about it."

"Oh, Mother, I love you!"

Sarah hugged Hannah again.

"I love you, too, Hannah! Now let us go in, get out of these Sunday dresses and set about keeping your promise not to disappoint Michael O'Brien with the first meal we cook for him."

CHAPTER FOURTEEN

Over the next several days, Caleb and O'Brien worked at cutting hay and taught Sarah and Hannah how to use the hay rakes. As the cut hay dried and the two ladies raked it, the two men took breaks from cutting to pitch the raked hay into the wagon as Sarah eased it along. Each time the wagon was filled, the men emptied it into the barn loft. Once the dried hay was up, they went back to cutting. When one meadow was cut, they moved on to another. Taking Saturday and Sunday off, O'Brien stayed to keep an eye on the ranch while the other three went to town for Hannah's piano lesson and church. By the middle of the following week, the barn loft was nearly full of hay, and they were working in the last meadow they planned to cut when the Swede rode up at a gallop.

"Folks, this is Lars Olsen; most everyone calls him Swede," O'Brien said by way of introduction. "Swede, what's your rush? That horse looks about done in."

"Frank Vickers is dead; he didn't come home last night, and we found him an hour ago on J H Connected range. Looks like the sharpshooter got him; must've thought he was one of your hands, Mrs. Hadley. I sent Billy Joe to bring George, and I came looking for you folks."

"Where was he goin'?" Caleb asked. "Or where had he been?"

"He was headed over to the Rafter M to try to convince old man Miller to loan us his wolfer for the hunting party he was trying to get together," Swede explained. "Don't know if he was still on the way over or on his way back."

"Did you tell Billy Joe to come back with a wagon, or do we need to take ours to get Frank home?" Sarah asked.

"I told him to bring one from the Slash V," Swede said. "I thought Frank deserved better than to be carried home lashed to his saddle."

"Miz Hadley, this prob'ly ain't somethin' you or Hannah needs to see," Caleb suggested. "Why don't I ride along with Swede to wait for George? O'Brien can see that you an' Hannah get home alright."

"Tell George to let me know if I can do anything for them," Sarah told him.

"O'Brien, you mind if we put Swede's saddle on your horse? You can drive the Hadleys back to the house, pick up another horse an' come along after us."

"Think I'll pick up my Sharps rifle and some cartridges while I'm there," O'Brien said. "If that fellow is still around, I might need it for us to have a chance against his Whitworth."

"Sounds like a good idee," Caleb agreed.

O'Brien stripped off his saddle and tossed it on the hay in the wagon. While Swede put his saddle on the fresher horse, O'Brien tied the spent horse to the back of the hay wagon.

"I'll see that he gets water and feed, Swede," O'Brien said. "You can pick him up later."

"Thanks, O'Brien," Swede said. "Took me a while to find where you all were working when I didn't find anyone at the ranch. I used the horse pretty hard; he deserves a rest."

"He'll get it," O'Brien said as he helped Sarah and Hannah into the wagon. "I'll catch up to you as quickly as I can, Caleb."

"You keep a sharp eye as you come," Caleb warned. "Frank was a big man hisself; that killer might have mistook him fer you."

"That's what I was thinking."

As O'Brien started the wagon south back to the J H Connected ranch house, Caleb followed Swede northeast to the place where he had found Frank Vickers' body. When the two riders arrived, Caleb took a close look at the wound that had killed Frank then he began to examine the ground for tracks or any signs that might tell him what had happened. Before long, he had a pretty good idea of what had happened, but he said nothing of what he found to Swede. He started a small fire and made a pot of coffee, then the two men sat on the ground with their full cups and waited for the others. George Vickers and the wagon from the Slash V were in sight but still a mile away when O'Brien rode up. Swede emptied his cup, put it in his saddlebag and climbed on his horse.

"Think I'll ride out and meet George," Swede said. "Don't know what he expects me to do, but I don't want him to think I'm doing nothing."

"You did all you could do, Swede," O'Brien assured him.

"Yep, nothing at all," Swede said wryly, as he spurred his horse toward the coming wagon.

"Take a look at Frank an' tell me what you think," Caleb said when Swede was far enough away not to hear.

One look was enough for O'Brien.

"Wasn't a Whitworth, probably wasn't a rifle," he said. "From the powder burns on his coat, I'd say it was a handgun from a few feet away."

"Looks to me like whoever he was ridin' with shot him in the back then led his horse in circles an' loops to make it look like the horse was grazin' before it finally headed off to the northwest an' back to the Slash V," Caleb said. "If we make a big circle after George an' the others head back to the Slash V with Frank, we might just be able to pick up the tracks of the killer who done this. But I'd say you're right; this wasn't the man that killed our hands

135

an' shot at Shiloh. Look around; there ain't no cover fer him to hide in. Nope, this was somebody diff'rent."

When the wagon arrived, George Vickers ordered Swede and Billy Joe to get his father's body loaded. He never touched his father, nor did he look around for signs of what had happened. He stayed on his horse and started them north without a word to Caleb or O'Brien. Swede held back, fiddling with his cinch until George had ridden away. When he mounted up, he spoke to O'Brien.

"Thanks, for the use of the horse. I'll return him when I can and pick up mine."

"We'll be at Frank's funeral," O'Brien said. "I'll ride over on your horse, and we can make the switch then. Don't say anything just yet, but I don't want to work for George, so I'll draw my time after the funeral and stay on at the J H Connected."

"That horse belongs to the Slash V; I don't own one. And I feel the same way as you about working for George," Swede admitted. "If Mrs. Hadley will take me on, just bring an extra horse, and I'll ride back with you."

"I'll vouch for you, and she needs hands," O'Brien told him. "So I'll bring an extra horse."

"Thanks," Swede said and rode away.

"Well," Caleb commented. "Looks like we're gatherin' the makin's of a cowboy crew. Reckon we better git that murderin' skunk before he decides he's got him a whole bunch of new targets."

"Yeah," O'Brien agreed. "But now we're looking for two murderin' skunks."

"Have a cup of coffee an' let's give them folks a chance to get out of sight," Caleb suggested. "Then we'll have a look fer tracks. Maybe this killer ain't as savvy as that sharpshooter."

Once the wagon and riders disappeared over a ridge, the two men put out the fire and started their search.

"Why don't we start over toward the Rafter M?" Caleb suggested. "That'll tell us whether Frank was comin' or goin'."

"If we split up, we can cover more ground," O'Brien offered. "If I find somethin' you need to look at, I'll wave my hat."

"Good idee," Caleb agreed. "I'll do the same."

The two men rode in opposite directions out about a quarter mile from the place where Frank had been shot then began to circle. Caleb rode southeast toward the Rafter M, and it took him less than half an hour to be certain that Frank had not gotten that far; he had already crossed the tracks of the Slash V wagon without finding any other tracks when he saw O'Brien wave his hat. He turned his horse and rode over.

"Back up that way," O'Brien said, pointing toward the place he had started his search near where the Slash V wagon had come and gone, "I found what I think was probably Frank's horse headed for the barn. The tracks weren't deep, and I believe I could see where the reins were dragging as the horse held his head out to the side to keep from stepping on them. We've got a different horse here, deeper tracks indicating a rider, and look at this hoofprint."

Caleb dismounted to look more closely.

"Looks like a nearly new shoe, but the inside end has a mighty noticeable gouge in it." Caleb walked along the path of the horse to look at other prints. "Purty big horse, long stride, the other shoes show some scratches, but nothin' like that gouge in the right hind shoe. You reckon the horse kicked at somethin' harder than the shoe, maybe a gate hinge or the like?"

"Could be," O'Brien agreed. "Let's see where the tracks lead."

They followed the tracks for half a mile before the trail turned northward; within another half mile they were agreed that the ridden horse was headed straight for Slash V range.

"Did you find any sign of where Frank come south?" Caleb asked.

"No," O'Brien told him. "I figured his tracks were covered by the horses Swede and Billy Joe rode following him."

"Let's ride back that way an' have another look," Caleb suggested. "I've got me a nasty hunch."

As they started that way, Caleb asked another question.

"Does George Vickers ride a string of horses? I can't remember that I've ever seen him ride anythin' but that big roan geldin' with the white blaze and four white stockin's."

"That's George's favorite. Frank was always getting on to him for not giving the horse enough rest. He never rides it at roundup or working the herd—afraid an ornery steer will hook him with a horn—but he rides it pretty much everywhere else. George always rides that roan when he goes visiting or to town."

"That fits with what I remember," Caleb said. "An' it might make my hunch work."

"You think George might have shot his own father in the back?"

"Yep."

When they reached the wagon tracks, both men dismounted and searched the ground for any track that showed the gouged shoe. It didn't take long to find several.

"Well," O'Brien said. "Only two saddle horses right at this point in the trail, and one of them belongs to the J H Connected; the other is George's roan, so it looks like your hunch is right. What do we do now?"

"I don't rightly know," Caleb said. "We need to get a look at the right hind shoe on that roan to be certain sure, then we need to git word to Dan Hobbs. Bein' town marshal, he cain't really do anythin' but send a letter to that worthless territorial marshal, but he still needs to know our suspicions. Fer certain, we ain't leavin' Miz Hadley or Hannah alone on the ranch or anywheres else 'til we see George behind bars or hung."

"I wish Shiloh was back," O'Brien said.

"Me, too," Caleb agreed.

* * * * * * *

Shiloh waited in Helena for three days to receive answers to all of his telegrams. Thomas Hadley and James Bancroft had gotten together and sent him one telegram with their combined knowledge of all ventures planned anywhere near the J H Connected. As Shiloh thought about what he had learned, he found himself disturbed by the prospect that the sharpshooter might be killing men in anticipation of making a fortune from a railroad project that had been canceled.

"Is it possible," he wondered. *"That this killer learned of the initial plans to build a railroad across the J H Connected range and doesn't know that the plans have been abandoned?"*

But there was nothing in the telegram to help him find the man, and the reply from Brent Madison simply told him to expect a package of information mailed to White Sulphur Springs and addressed to Sarah Hadley. During the wait, Shiloh had bought the pair of Angora chaps Caleb had suggested he would need for the winter, along with an extra set of wool longjohns, a pair of heavy wool britches, two wool shirts and a fur trapper's hat with earflaps. The weather was turning bitter as he saddled his horse to leave Helena, so he put on the heavy wool britches, an extra shirt under his sheepskin coat and the 'woolie' chaps. He looked at the sky as he rode out of the livery barn and prayed it wouldn't snow; he wanted to get back to the J H Connected as soon as he could; snow would slow him down for certain and might force a long detour if it closed Duck Creek Pass.

* * * * * * *

Caleb, O'Brien and the Hadleys finished haying the day after Frank Vickers was found dead. When they returned to the ranch with the last wagonload of hay, Sarah found a note pushed under the front door telling them that Frank's funeral was to be held the following afternoon at the Slash V ranch headquarters.

"Okay," Caleb said. "We'll go to the funeral an' hope Dan Hobbs shows up. Don't know why he come to Shiloh's when he didn't come to any of the other funerals out here. Might've had something to do with them letters bein' wrote. If he ain't at Frank's, one of us needs to tell the preacher to pass the word to him about our suspicions that George killed his pappy. Miz Hadley, it might be easiest fer you to do that."

"I should not have any problem getting a private word with Reverend Reardon," Sarah agreed. "I can certainly tell Ann."

"I'd appreciate it if you an' Hannah would stay together an' always in sight of either me or O'Brien. George is sure to want to talk to you alone, so you might have to be rude to him to do that."

"I shall try not to be rude," she said. "But I have no intentions of going anywhere alone with George Vickers."

"O'Brien, you prob'ly have the best chance to get a look at the shoe on George's roan," Caleb said. "So I guess I should be the one to keep an eye on our womenfolk."

"It might be wise not to tell Swede what we think George has done," O'Brien said. "At least not until we're on our way back here. I don't know how good he is at hiding his feelings, and he worked for Frank for a long time. He might even decide to go after George himself. He could likely handle George, but I doubt that he's a match for any of the new men George has been hiring, and I'd hate to see him get killed."

"You're prob'ly right about that," Caleb agreed.

"Can either of you think of something more we can do?" Sarah asked.

"We can pick our route carefully, maybe come back a different way than we go an' watch our backtrail both ways," Caleb said. "If the sharpshooter is a killer hired by George, he might be out huntin' tomorrow. Might be, anyhow."

"Caleb, I am worried about Shiloh riding into this without knowing what has happened," Sarah said. "And I cannot think of any way to get word to him. When do you expect him back?"

"Could be back anytime now, Miz Hadley, but the weather's turnin' cold. If it snows, 'specially in the mountains, it could slow him considerable. But I wouldn't worry about him runnin' into somethin' unexpected; about now he's as wary as a wild horse when there's ropes around."

Hannah had been silent through all of the planning; now she walked over and wrapped her arms around Caleb's waist.

"Caleb, I'm a little frightened; I don't want anything to happen to you."

"Hannah, I'm just a little scared my own self," Caleb admitted. "But God will look after us, an' if he decides to call me home, now or ten years from now, you can be sure we'll be together in heaven when he calls you home."

"What about you, Mr. O'Brien?" Hannah asked. "If God calls any of us home, will you be with us in heaven when it's your time to die?"

"I guess I don't know how to answer that, Hannah," O'Brien told her truthfully. "Shiloh tried to explain to me what it means to have eternal life, but I didn't fully understand, and we planned to talk again when he gets back. But he did tell me that anyone here, and maybe especially you, could help me to understand what it means to truly be saved."

"Then the most important thing we need to do before tomorrow," Hannah said. "Is to make sure that you understand and *are* truly saved. I don't want you protecting me until I know God is protecting you."

"Amen to that," Caleb agreed.

"Well, you've got your work cut out for you, young lady," O'Brien said ruefully. "I reckon I'm the next thing to a heathen."

"It's really not hard at all, and God does all the work," Hannah told him. "Salvation is a free gift, and you only have to understand your need for it and be willing to ask for and accept it on God's terms. Jesus died a horrible death to pay the price for our sins, so that we can have eternal life."

Without knowing that she was repeating much of what Shiloh had told Michael O'Brien, and with the prayers and occasional comments of Sarah and Caleb supporting her efforts, Hannah Hadley explained to him what it meant to be repentant for sinfulness and how to accept the free gift of salvation. Before they sat down for supper that night, Michael O'Brien knew for certain that he had received the gift of eternal life.

CHAPTER FIFTEEN

The following morning at breakfast, Caleb asked Sarah if he should hitch the team to the wagon or the carriage.

"You an' Hannah will ride easier in the carriage, but, if you think we need a last list of supplies before the snow comes, we could start early an' swing by Jenkins' store on the way to the Slash V. That way we could come straight home from the funeral an' might make it in before full dark. An' I might catch Dan Hobbs in town, so I could tell him our suspicions about George."

"That is a good idea, Caleb," Sarah agreed. "We shall need supplies for the two new hands. I was thinking we would take the wagon when we go in for church, but from the looks of the sky this morning, we may not be able to make it in on Saturday or Sunday."

The lean old man excused himself from the table and retrieved his hat.

I'll be in the barn when you're done eatin' Miz Hadley out of house an' home," Caleb said to O'Brien. "Might be, we ought to take two wagons to haul enough supplies to feed you through the winter."

O'Brien gave Caleb an exaggerated wink and a huge grin.

"It might take me several lifetimes to get my fill of the food in *this* kitchen. So I'll just finish off this last dozen biscuits to tide me over, then I'll be coming along right behind you."

Caleb did not see any dozen biscuits left on the table, but he had no doubts that the big Irishman could eat that many. He just shook his head and smiled at O'Brien.

"See you in the barn."

As Caleb disappeared through the back door, Sarah decided a comment from her was in order.

"You do know Caleb was just teasing you, I hope."

"That I do, ma'am," O'Brien assured her. "I hope that old man thinks as much of me as I do him."

"I am certain he does," she said. "And I do not want you to ever feel bashful about eating your fill. You are a very large man; you work very hard, and we are very grateful that you have come to help us."

"Thank you, ma'am," O'Brien said earnestly. "It's nice to be appreciated." He excused himself and grabbed his own hat. "I truly hate for there to be leftovers of such good food. But, if I don't get on down to the barn, Caleb will have the team hitched to the wagon and both horses saddled before I get there. That old man can get more done with less effort than any man I've ever known, and, if there's any laziness about him, he sure doesn't let it show."

As O'Brien walked past Hannah on the way to the door, she handed him a buttered biscuit.

"Just so you don't faint from hunger between the house and the barn," she snickered.

O'Brien bent down and kissed her on the forehead.

"Lassie, now that you've shown me the path to eternal life, you're going to have to bake a lot of biscuits. Forever is a long time."

"Man does not live by bread alone," Hannah quoted in her best patriarchal voice.

"No, but that doesn't mean an Irish lad can't take saintly pleasure in hot buttered biscuits," he said as he ruffled her hair.

Hannah watched O'Brien walk down the back steps chewing the biscuit she had given him then she turned to her mother.

"Mr. O'Brien was already a nice man before he was saved; it's going to be fun to watch him grow up in the Lord."

"Yes," Sarah agreed. "I think it will. But we need to be certain to remember him in our prayers. He will be facing spiritual attacks now as well as attacks from the man who has been shooting our people."

"Last night seemed so very special to me. I'd never helped anyone come to Jesus before. I couldn't have done it without you and Caleb," Hannah admitted. "But it was wonderful to be a part of it."

"It was a very special night, and you allowed God to use you in the most important work we can do in this life. I was very proud of you, and heaven was rejoicing over Michael O'Brien."

"Mother, is it wrong for me to want the man who's been doing the shooting stopped, even if it means someone will have to kill him?"

"It is not wrong to seek justice, nor to pray for it," Sarah told her. "Our laws, which would put this man to death for murder, are based on God's law, which says that death is the appropriate penalty for some sins or crimes. But it *is* wrong to seek revenge."

"How do I know the difference between justice and revenge?" Hannah asked.

"If this murderer is killed while attacking us, that would be self-defense or defense of innocent people, and that is just. If he is captured and put to death by the courts, that, too, is just. But if we captured him, tortured him just to make him suffer then killed him, that would be revenge. If we killed him then put his family to death, even though they were innocent, that would be revenge. If we burned down the town he lived in or a ranch he lived on simply because he lived there, even though his neighbors knew nothing of his evil deeds, that, too, would be revenge."

"Is it something like the destruction of Sodom and Gomorrah?

Not even ten righteous people could be found, only four, so Lot, his wife and daughters were saved, but the cities were destroyed. Destruction of the guilty was justice, but not to save the righteous would have been taking revenge on them for their neighbors' sins."

"That is the principle, Hannah," Sarah told her. "The New Testament does tell us that Lot was righteous; I cannot dispute that, though I would question his righteousness without Peter's statements. But the Bible does not tell us that his wife or his daughters were righteous, and their actions lead me to believe they were not. I believe they were shown compassion either for Lot's sake or because they were Abraham's kinsmen, and Abraham was righteous."

"So they escaped justice and received mercy because of Lot or Abraham in the same way we escape punishment for our sins and receive eternal life because of Jesus?"

"I had never thought it through that far," Sarah said. "And Lot's wife did not escape because of disobedience. But, where his daughters are concerned, I believe that is exactly right."

"What about turning the other cheek when struck by one who is evil? Are we to let this evil man shoot us?"

"I do not believe so, Hannah," Sarah said. "A slap on the cheek is not life-threatening, and the teaching Jesus gives in that sermon is about attitudes of the heart. We are not to return evil for evil. But one of the last instructions Jesus gave to his disciples included buying a sword. When Peter used his in the garden of Gethsemane, he was rebuked for using it at the wrong time. Most of the apostles were put to death for their faith, and we may be asked to suffer in the same way. But being willing to die for the cause of Christ does not mean we should allow evil to go unchallenged."

"How will I know when to give myself willingly and when to resist? We've been practicing with our rifles and revolvers ever since Shiloh told us to. How will we know when to use them?"

"I truly do not know, honey," Sarah admitted. "I believe we must pray earnestly that we never need to use them, and that we must trust God to tell us if we should."

Hannah just nodded and hugged her mother, but Sarah could tell she was still greatly troubled by her uncertainties and conflicting thoughts.

"Come on, honey," Sarah said gently. "We should pack our dresses for the funeral. We can change when we get to the Slash V. We shall need warmer clothes for the trip."

"This time I think we should take our swords with us," Hannah said quietly.

"Then we shall."

* * * * * * *

Caleb was slightly surprised to find rifles, revolvers and cartridges wrapped in a blanket next to the luggage, but he said nothing. He had brought his "swords," and in addition to carrying his sidearm, O'Brien had put his buffalo rifle in the wagon. As Caleb and the Hadleys stepped out onto the front porch, Sarah noticed that O'Brien was mounted on the Slash V horse Swede had left and had two unsaddled horses tied to the back of the wagon. One wore the J H Connected brand, the second was the Slash V horse O'Brien had ridden the day of the false funeral.

"Mr. O'Brien, when you tell George you are drawing your time, be sure to tell him I will pay your wages for the time you have been loaned to us," she said. "It is only fair that I should, and it may make things easier for both you and Lars Olsen."

"Yes, ma'am," O'Brien said.

"Mr. Olsen seems like a good man," Sarah said. "He must also be a brave man to be willing to come to work on this ranch at this time."

"Ma'am, if Swede had been here when folks started dying, he'd either still be here, or he'd be dead," O'Brien told her.

"And I suspect the same thing could be said of you."

"Yes, ma'am, I suspect so.

"Well, I pray neither of you gets killed."

"If I do now, we know we'll see each other again, so we need to pray especially for Swede until we can share the good news of the gospel with him."

"Amen to that," Caleb agreed.

The temperature was well below freezing, and the sun was hidden by low, gray clouds. After Caleb had placed the bags and blanket-wrapped firearms in the wagon, he pulled his buffalo coat off of his saddle and slipped into it. He was already wearing his pair of the "woolie" chaps he had recommended to Shiloh; he tied a wool scarf around his ears and the lower part of his face, donned a fur hat and heavy mittens. Then he mounted up.

O'Brien did not own a pair of the angora chaps; he wore elkhide, but between them and his longjohns he wore two pairs of heavy wool trousers and two heavy wool shirts under his wool mackinaw coat. He had tied his hat on with his neckerchief so that the wool felt brim was pulled down over his ears, and he wore thick leather gloves.

Sitting next to her mother on the wagon seat, Hannah had wrapped a blanket around her winter clothes, and she held another around her mother and snuggled against her as Sarah started the team toward town. It would be a long, cold day for the travelers.

* * * * * * *

When they reached White Sulphur Springs, Sarah stopped the team next to the boardwalk in front of Jenkins' store. Caleb and O'Brien hitched their horses to the rail and helped the ladies down.

"O'Brien, you mind stayin' with our womenfolk an' seein' that the supplies git loaded proper, while I go hunt up Dan Hobbs?" Caleb asked.

"Go ahead, and take your time. If we get the wagon loaded before you get back, you'll find me wrapped around the stove inside the store trying to soak up enough heat to keep me warm until I can get back to my post guarding that pot-bellied stove in the bunkhouse on the J H Connected."

"Cold ride into town fer you, was it?" Caleb asked in mock surprise. "Reminded me of a pleasant spring mornin'."

"I'm too much a gentleman to call you a liar," O'Brien retorted. "But I don't believe a word of that tall tale."

Caleb grunted at him and headed toward the town marshal's office. Inside the store, Sarah and Hannah were already gathering things from the supplies list, and O'Brien was surprised to find Smoke minding the store.

"Not going to this funeral, Smoke?" he asked.

"Mr. Frank neveh had no use fo' me, an' Ah ain't got no use fo' Mr. George," Smoke said. "Boss man done went by hisself this time."

"Well, let me look at that list; I'll help you load the wagon. Sooner we get rolling again, sooner we get this day over, and I can get back to a warm fire."

"Don' like the cold weather?"

"Not particularly."

"Ah does," Smoke told him. "Ah likes it real well, 'cept Ah cain't fish when the streams is froze."

"Sure you can," O'Brien said. "You can cut a hole in the ice on the frozen lakes. I can teach you when we get caught up on the J H Connected."

"Ah'd sho' appreciate that, but won' you hate fishin' in the cold?"

"You can stay out in the cold if you want to; I'll be building myself a shelter and making a heater to go inside it."

* * * * * * *

Caleb found Dan Hobbs at his desk. After he had told the marshal everything he and O'Brien knew or suspected, the lawman considered what he had heard before he spoke.

"Well, I cain't go out to the Slash V and arrest George; I got no jurisdiction outside of town. But, if you or O'Brien can get a look at that horseshoe and are willing to swear out statements that it's the same horse, I can arrest George the next time he comes to town and hold him in jail on suspicion of murder until the territorial marshal and the circuit judge can come out here to hold a trial," Hobbs said. "What I cain't figure out is what George is after that is worth so much to him that he'd be willin' to kill his own pa. And, if he did hire this rifleman that's shootin' the J H Connected cowboys, what's the J H Connected got that he don't already have on the Slash V?"

"Might be, the answer to both questions is Sarah Hadley," Caleb suggested.

"I guess that could be," Hobbs admitted. "But it don't make no sense. Mrs. Hadley's been a widow for, what, two years now? Why wouldn't George just go courtin' and ask her to marry him?"

"Well, he's been to the house several times an' talked to her in town an' at church," Caleb said. "Might be, that's his idee of courtin', an' maybe he has asked her to marry him. Maybe she told him no an' never mentioned it to me. She knows I don't like George, an' it ain't none of my business, nohow."

"Maybe you should ask her," Hobbs suggested. "It'd help to know."

"I think I will," Caleb agreed. "If she tells me to mind my own business, she'll be nice about it."

"If one of you can get a look at George's roan, get word to me one way or the other."

"One of us, prob'ly Miz Hadley, will send word with the preacher."

CHAPTER SIXTEEN

As soon as the J H Connected group arrived at the Slash V, O'Brien took the two Slash V horses and the spare J H Connected horse into the barn. He quickly switched his saddle to the J H Connected horse, and he was rubbing down the Slash V horse he had ridden when Swede walked into the barn.

"I brought an extra mount for me," O'Brien said. "Figured you'll have made friends by now with that horse you borrowed, so you can ride him back to the J H Connected."

"He's a good horse," Swede said. "Shows a lot of heart, a real willingness to work."

"Then start your string with him," O'Brien offered.

"Thanks, I will. I'll go ahead and throw my saddle on him, so you folks won't have to wait on me when it's time to leave."

"Good idea," O'Brien agreed. "Isn't that George's roan in the corner stall? Always admired that horse; never cared for the way George used him," he said as he walked toward the stall.

"Neither did Frank, but George never paid much attention to the old man where that horse was concerned."

O'Brien eased into the stall and began to rub the roan's neck.

He talked to the gelding gently and worked it around so that its hindquarters were toward the nearest lantern then he reached down and lifted the right hind hoof. He felt the shoe with his fingers then ducked down for a quick look. It was the gouged shoe he was looking for. As he straightened up, Swede called over to him.

"You know George don't like anyone fooling with that horse."

The big Irishman grinned at him. As he stepped out of the stall he saw the roan's prints in the dirt of the barn floor. He looked back up and responded to Swede's statement.

"What's he going to do, fire me? I'm going to unhitch the wagon team and bring them in out of the cold. When you get that saddle cinched, would you bring Caleb's horse in?"

"Be glad to."

* * * * * * *

The funeral at the Slash V was a brief and bitterly cold affair. Because of the wind, few of those present were able to hear much of the eulogy or prayers. And it was difficult for O'Brien to pass on his discovery; he had planned to simply whisper in Sarah's ear. Instead, he wrote a note on a page in his tally book with the stub of a pencil he carried, tore the page out and slipped it into Sarah's hand. When the service was over, Sarah waited until O'Brien and Swede had George engaged in paying their final wages. Then she led the minister next to one of the outbuildings to a place sheltered from the wind. She looked about carefully for anyone who might overhear before she spoke.

"Pastor, when you get back to town, please stop in at the marshal's office on your way home and tell him the tracks that Caleb spoke to him about were definitely made by George Vickers' roan horse. He will understand the significance of your report."

"May I know what this is about?" he asked.

"The marshal will explain," she said. "But it is very important

152

that no one overhear our conversation."

"I understand, and I will deliver your message to Dan."

"Thank you," Sarah said. "I have not seen Ann yet, and we shall be leaving soon. If I miss her, please give her my love."

"I persuaded her not to come," Reardon told her. "The sky looks like we could get snow at any time, and I was reluctant to make the trip in the buggy, so I rode out with Mr. Jenkins in his wagon."

"That was probably a wise decision and certainly one Frank would have understood. He was not a sentimental man, or did not seem to be, but he was very thoughtful where we women were concerned."

"Yes, he was, and Ann remembers that." He shook his head sadly. "I've prayed for Frank Vickers many times over the years I've known him. He was a good man in many ways, but I cannot say that I was ever able to make him understand that he, like all of us, needed to recognize his shortcomings, repent, ask for and receive forgiveness and eternal salvation. I greatly fear, now that it is too late, Frank fully understands the consequences of that failure."

"It must be very hard for you to speak at a funeral and try to console the family of a person you believe to be unsaved."

"It is extremely difficult, even painful," he admitted. "I can't lie to the family, the only hope I can offer is that God is just and merciful, and that only He can truly know what is in a person's heart."

"That cannot be of much consolation if the family understands that each of us justly deserves eternal punishment and must humbly and with a repentant spirit ask for God's mercy in order to receive it."

"No, I'm afraid it isn't," he agreed. "In this case I fear George has as little understanding as his father did, and I'm afraid my words are foolishness to him."

"Well, we can continue to pray for him," Sarah said. "So long as he lives, there is hope for him, even if it is too late for his father."

Sarah's statement stirred Reardon's curiosity, but, before he thought of a tactful way to word the question that troubled him, Caleb walked up.

"Team's hitched to the wagon, Miz Hadley. An' O'Brien an' the Swede should be just about done with their business."

"Thank you, Caleb," Sarah said. "Pastor, please remember to deliver my message on your way home. I believe it to be very urgent."

"I will, Mrs. Hadley," the minister assured her. "I do have my failings, but forgetfulness is not one of them, at least not yet. Perhaps, it will become so as I grow older." Reardon shook hands with both Sarah and Caleb. "I trust you'll have a safe trip back to your ranch."

O'Brien and Swede were coming toward them as they reached the wagon. Because of the bitter cold and the lateness of their arrival, Sarah and Hannah had not changed from their traveling clothes, so both were ready to leave. Caleb helped Sarah climb up to sit beside Hannah; he could see that George had seen her and was coming her way.

"I'll git my horse," he said. "But I'll be close by."

Seeing Caleb walk away, O'Brien led Swede toward him. Caleb met them at the barn door and waited outside where he could watch George while the other two brought out the three saddle horses. As he mounted up, he asked how things had gone with George.

"If he was upset by anything," O'Brien said. "It was parting with our wages."

"That figures," Caleb said. "Let's ease on over by the wagon so Miz Hadley can break away from him."

As they reached the wagon, they could hear George asking Sarah to stay and visit for a while.

"Thank you for the invitation, George, and please accept my

heartfelt condolences for the loss of your father. I hope you will not think me terribly rude and unfeeling, but I must leave. The weather looks like we may have snow soon, and we need to get home before it does. Even if it does not snow, we shall be hard-pressed to reach the ranch before dark."

Without giving him a chance to argue, she stirred up the team and turned them toward the J H Connected. Once they were away from the buildings, Swede rode up beside the wagon.

"Mrs. Hadley, would you mind if I spend the night in town and report for work in the morning? Now that I've been paid, I need a few things from the store before winter settles in to stay."

"That is fine, Mr. Olsen," Sarah told him. "If you do not have quite enough for everything you need, have the clerk put the balance on the ranch account, and we shall consider it an advance on your wages."

The two were practically shouting to be heard over the wind, so O'Brien was able to hear the conversation. He rode up next to Swede and handed him the wages he had drawn from the Slash V.

"Use what you need of this," he said. "But don't tell anyone either of us has moved to the J H Connected just yet. We're trying to keep that sharpshooter from finding out for as long as possible."

"Thanks, O'Brien," Swede told him. "I'll bring back what I don't need, and I'll keep my mouth shut."

"Have a drop of Irish whiskey on me, lad, but stay sober," O'Brien warned. "And when you ride out of town to the ranch, be alert and try to stay in open country well clear of trees or cover that murdering madman might hide in or behind. If visibility is good and the wind is still, the rifle he's shooting will reach out beyond a mile, and he's already shown the skill to use it at 800 yards. So don't fall asleep in the saddle."

"I won't," Swede promised, as he waved and veered off toward town.

"That was very generous of you Mr. O'Brien," Sarah said. "And very wise. I am afraid I forgot for a moment how careful and closed-mouth we need to be at this time."

"Some lessons are hard learned and never forgotten, ma'am," he said. "The war's been over more than ten years, but General Clifton trained me well, and war isn't the only danger we face in life, so I've not lost my caution."

"General Clifton? Oh, you mean, Shiloh!" She laughed at herself. "I am afraid I am not accustomed to hearing him called by his real name. I hope one day soon he will be comfortable using it again."

"Yes ma'am, me too."

CHAPTER SEVENTEEN

Shiloh was lost. He had spent the night in the north line cabin on the J H Connected and started out at first light. Then it had begun to snow heavily, and the landmarks looked different. Under the bleak sky and with the wind swirling the snow around him, it was difficult for him to get his bearings. He climbed down from his horse and dug into his saddlebags for his compass. He knew he was north of the ranch, east of the Smith River and west of the trail to White Sulphur Springs. So he only had to figure out where south was, head in that direction until he reached the curve of the river or Agate Creek, and he could find his way.

With the compass to guide him, he remounted and started south. He had ridden less than a mile when he spotted a saddled horse and a man lying in the snow. He stopped his horse and studied the situation. The snow was still falling, but the flakes were smaller and fewer than they had been. He knew he was in open country, but visibility was still less than one hundred feet. The falling snow would have dampened the sound of a rifle shot, but he would still have heard one fired nearby. If the man on the ground was another victim of the shooter Shiloh sought, he had probably been shot before it began to snow. And the sharpshooter was likely long gone.

Shiloh thought he recognized the chestnut gelding; when he

reached him and settled him down, he confirmed that he wore a J H Connected brand. The rider had the reins wrapped around his left hand and had fallen with his body pinning the hand and reins beneath him, so the horse had not pulled free. Shiloh thought he recognized the rider as someone he had seen, but he did not know him and had no idea why he had been riding a J H Connected horse.

When Shiloh knelt down beside the man, he was surprised to discover that he was breathing. He had been shot in the back, through the left side below the shoulder blade. But he had not been shot with a Whitworth rifle. Gripping the reins to keep the horse from running away, Shiloh lifted and turned the unconscious man until he could see that the bullet had gone all the way through and come out a little higher than it had gone in.

"He was either leaning forward in the saddle," Shiloh thought. *"Or he was shot from below, perhaps by a man standing on the ground."*

Shiloh could see that he had fallen before the snow began to fall, which meant he had been on the ground for several hours.

"The cold probably kept him from bleeding to death," Shiloh thought. *"But he's not far from freezing to death. He isn't wearing a coat,"* Shiloh realized. *"He must have left somewhere in a big hurry."*

Shiloh was closer to the stocked cave than he was to the ranch buildings and decided to take the man there, so he could get him sheltered and near a warm fire as quickly as possible. He was still not certain of his exact position, but he figured he could find the cave by riding east to the broken foothills of the Castle Mountains and skirting the edges until he was in the trees that hid the cave.

Still holding the reins, Shiloh lifted the man and laid him across the saddle then he tied him in place. He led the chestnut to his bay, mounted, checked his compass and started east. He had traveled only a few minutes, praying for the man as he rode and asking God to help him find the cave, when the snow stopped. As he continued east, he began to see patches of blue sky to the north and northwest as the wind blew the storm beyond him. By the time he reached the foothills, he could see well enough to know exactly where he was, and he rode straight to the cave.

Tying the horses to tree branches near the cave mouth, he untied the man, carried him to the cave opening then dragged him through the low entrance to the ring of rocks and began to build a fire. Once the fire was going, Shiloh put a pot of water on to boil then made a bed of boughs and laid a couple of blankets over them. He removed the wounded man's boots and lifted him onto the blankets, laying him on his right side. He wrapped the blankets over the man's legs and lower body then used his hunting knife to cut away the man's vest and shirt to expose the entry and exit wounds.

While he was waiting for the water to boil, he pulled out some of the cloths he and Caleb had packed in for bandages. Still waiting for the water to boil, he held his knife blade in the flames to heat the blade, being careful not to let the blade become covered in soot. Then he went outside and searched the wounded man's saddlebags until he found a small silver flask. Unscrewing the cap, he took a sniff; he recognized the smell of whiskey and was surprised when he was not tempted to take a sip.

"Thank you, Lord," he said aloud.

Returning to the cave with the flask, the man's canteen and both the man's saddlebags and his own, he found the water boiling. He tore two squares of cloth and dropped them into the boiling water. Using the knife tip, he made sure both were fully immersed and left the cloths in the boiling water while he rummaged among the food supplies. He put another smaller pot of water on to boil and dug into his own saddlebags to get some of the jerked beef he had bought in Helena the day he left.

Then he knelt down beside the man and lifted one of the cloths out of the boiling water with the knife blade. When the cloth was cool enough to touch, he held it by two corners, folded it into a pad and began cleaning the exit wound. When done, he repeated the process with the second cloth and cleaned the entry wound. The man began to stir as he worked around the wounds. When he poured whiskey from the flask liberally over and into both wounds, the man flinched and groaned aloud, but he did not open his eyes. Taking more cloth, Shiloh made bandages for the wounds and held them in place by lengths of cloth tied around the man's ribs. Then he covered his upper body with the blankets.

By the time Shiloh was finished doing what little he knew to do for the wounds, the second pot of water was boiling. He dropped a piece of jerked beef into the pot, eased the pot to the edge of the fire to simmer and added several sticks to the fire. Then he took the first pot from the fire and put on his coffee pot. When the simmering jerky had turned the water into beef broth, he stirred a can of tomatoes into the pot and left it to continue simmering.

Shiloh sat on the cave floor close to the fire, poured himself a cup of coffee and looked closely at the man. His face was very pale beneath a stubble of blonde beard, but his nose and ears did not appear to be frostbitten. Shiloh did not know if the bullet had gone through his lung, but he did not see blood on his lips and had not heard air sucking into the wounds. He thought the bullet had broken at least one rib and probably two. He thought maybe the ribs had deflected the bullet away from the man's lung.

Shiloh was not certain there was a doctor in White Sulphur Springs, but the man needed to be taken to one, which might mean taking him to Fort Benton. Either way, he would need to be taken by wagon. Shiloh was trying to decide whether to leave him now and ride to the ranch to bring back a wagon or wait to see if he would wake up, when the man opened his eyes and looked directly at him.

"Who are you?" the man asked, his voice weak and wheezing.

"Folks call me Shiloh."

"I thought you were dead," the man said. "Am I dead?"

"Neither of us is dead," Shiloh assured him. "The man who

shot at me missed; the one who shot at you didn't, so be still, the bullet went through your left side."

"George Vickers shot me," he said. "Right after he shot the town marshal."

"The marshal dead?"

"He was still shooting at George and a couple of his gunhands when I lit a shuck. Don't know how it ended."

His statement ended in a bout of coughing. Shiloh knew he should let the wounded man rest, but he needed information, so he pressed his interrogation.

"What was the shooting about?"

"I guess the marshal was trying to arrest George and somebody started shooting. I'd spent the night in the livery stable hayloft and was saddling up to head out to the J H Connected, when I heard shooting across the street at the store. The horse whinnied; George realized I'd seen him and started shooting at me." The man paused, his pain evident and his breathing raspy. "I wasn't near my gun; it was with my bedroll and coat. So I jumped in the saddle and took out the back door of the barn. George managed to get a slug into me before I turned the corner." The man looked around the cave, trying to see beyond the flickering light of the fire. "I remember starting out for the ranch, but nothing after. Where am I?"

"In a cave on the ranch," Shiloh told him. "I found you an hour or so ago. I was lost myself at the time. Why was the marshal trying to arrest George?"

"I don't know unless he thinks George is the one who killed his poppa."

"Frank Vickers is dead?"

"Yep, I found him, well, Billy Joe and I did. We thought the same fellow killed him as killed all the J H Connected hands." Another bout of coughing and wheezing interrupted his tale. "We found Frank on Hadley range, and O'Brien thought the bullet might have been meant for him. Frank loaned O'Brien to Mrs. Hadley to help Caleb bring her hay in for the winter; O'Brien thought the killer might have found out and come after him. With Frank dead, we both drew our time after the funeral yesterday and hired on with Mrs. Hadley."

"What's your name?" Shiloh asked.

"Lars Olsen, but folks call me Swede."

"Well, Swede, I'd better let you rest; the talking isn't doing you any good. I brought your canteen in, and I made some broth with beef jerky and tomatoes. I think it's probably safe for you to have some broth or a drink of water."

"My mouth's real dry, let me have some water first."

Shiloh supported his head and shoulders and held the canteen to his lips while he drank. When he had had enough, Shiloh spoonfed some of the broth to him from the soup he had made. He was giving Swede another drink of water when they heard shooting in the distance.

CHAPTER EIGHTEEN

"It isn't like Swede to be late," O'Brien told Caleb as the two sat by the pot-bellied stove in the bunkhouse.

"He might've got turned around in the heavy snowfall this mornin'," Caleb said. "Or he might've holed up somewhere to wait it out. Couldn't hardly see past the nose on yore face when we went up fer breakfast. Now that the sky's cleared up, he'll prob'ly be along soon."

"Well, I know we need to get started cutting firewood," O'Brien said. "But if he doesn't show up before noon, I think I ought to go look for him after we eat."

Before Caleb could reply, they heard the sound of running horses. O'Brien jumped up, opened the door a crack and peeked out.

"Better grab hold of your Spencer, Caleb," he said. "It's George Vickers and four of those extra hands he hired, and it doesn't look like a social call."

The five Slash V riders charged toward the ranch house at a gallop, their horses sliding to a stop at the porch.

"Val, Slade, find O'Brien and that old man and kill them! If Swede's here, kill him, too!" George shouted. "Slim, Ryan, come with me!"

Sarah and Hannah were in the root cellar putting away the last of the new supplies when they heard the running horses. They heard the shouting but could not make out the words.

"Stay here, Hannah," Sarah said as she started up the stairs. She reached the top step just as George and his two gunmen burst through the front door.

"Get Hannah and pack some clothes," George ordered. "I'm taking you to the Slash V!"

"You know, George," Sarah said calmly. "It is customary to knock and wait until you have been invited in. What do you mean by charging through my front door like a stampeding cattle herd? And why would I want to pack and accompany you to the Slash V?"

"Don't play coy with me, Sarah Hadley!" George was still shouting. "I've wanted you from the first time I saw you, and you've been a widow for two years. Now it's time we were married. With our ranches combined, we'll have White Sulphur Springs surrounded, and we'll own our own small empire. I'm taking over the town; it'll be our headquarters, our capitol. We'll have our own army. I'll be king of the Castle Mountain country, and you'll be my queen!"

Sarah stared at him in disbelief, shocked by his words. She struggled to maintain her calm demeanor.

"George, we do not have kings and queens in this territory; one day, we will be a State with a President and a Congress. And you cannot make the town your headquarters. People live there, have homes, own businesses."

"Anyone who wants to work for me can stay," George shouted sharply. "I'll run the rest out. Now get packed; I've waited long enough to make you my wife!"

"George Vickers, I have no intentions of marrying you now or ever. Are you insane?"

As Sarah asked the question, she saw the look of rage sweep across his face and realized that George Vickers truly was insane.

Sarah saw the blow coming and tried to duck out of the way; instead of a backhand slap across the face, George struck the side of her neck with his forearm and the full force of his rage. Sarah was unconscious before she hit the floor. George drew his handgun and pointed it at the fallen woman.

"If you won't marry *me*, Sarah," he said very softly. "You'll never again marry anyone."

"Boss," Ryan said from beside him. "Didn't none of us hire on to be killin' no womenfolk."

Hannah had picked up her revolver from the shelf in front of the tunnel entrance and crept up the root cellar stairs. Her eyes cleared the top step in time to see George strike her mother. As he drew his gun, Hannah lifted hers and aimed at his heart. When Ryan spoke, George turned, fully intending to shoot Ryan; the move saved his life. Hannah's bullet struck the cylinder of his gun, deflected upward through his right arm and caused him to drop his weapon.

"Leave now, Mr. Vickers," Hannah told him. "Or I *will* shoot you again!"

Ryan had drawn his own weapon and was also aiming at George.

"Hold your fire, little lady," he said. "We're goin'. Slim, outside. George, go on, git, or I'll shoot you myself."

Sarah had lit a lamp that morning to dispel the grayness of the storm. Because she and Hannah had spent the morning in the root cellar, the lamp was still burning. As George walked by the sidetable where it sat, he grabbed the lamp and flung it against the far wall of the parlor. The lamp shattered against a window and burning oil splattered across the drapes and wall. An upholstered chair in front of the window ignited, and the dry lumber in the wall was soon blazing.

Outside, Val and Slade were riding slowly toward the barn and bunkhouse. Caleb was circling to reach the back door of the house; O'Brien was covering him from the bunkhouse. When O'Brien heard gunfire from the house, he fired two well-aimed shots at Val and Slade and knocked both men out of their saddles. Loading the single-shot Sharps for a third time from the row of cartridges he had placed on the floor beside him, O'Brien waited while Caleb ran for the house, carrying his Spencer at the ready. Moments later, three men came out the front door onto the porch, and O'Brien fired again, missing Slim, who dived off the porch and crawled into the drifted snow against the stone foundation of the house to take cover. As he peeked around the corner to see if he could locate O'Brien, he saw Caleb running toward the back of the house. Slim fired three quick shots; the second one hit Caleb in the left thigh and knocked him down.

Ryan, under fire, abandoned his plan to secure George then go back to get the Hadleys out of the burning house; instead, he jumped over the porch banister and ran for his horse. George ran down the porch steps barely a stride behind him and raced for his roan.

Caleb had no cover where he fell and began to crawl toward the well behind the house, leaving a blood red streak as he dragged his wounded leg across the white blanket of snow. O'Brien saw the running men and set the crosshairs of his telescopic sight on George's head.

"No, mister," he said to himself. "I'm going to save you for the judge."

O'Brien lowered his aim and shot George through the left leg. As George tried to pull himself up by his stirrup, O'Brien reloaded and shot him through the right leg. The roan pulled away and started running for the Slash V. Ryan leaped into his saddle and spurred his horse toward the aspen trees surrounding the beaver pond. O'Brien let him go. Slim, who still had a clear shot at Caleb, saw Shiloh charging toward the house with his bay at a dead run and threw his gun into the snow.

"I quit!" he yelled. "I give up!"

O'Brien ran from the bunkhouse toward the house with his

Sharps rifle in his left hand and his Remington revolver in his right.

"Caleb," he yelled. "Are you alright?"

"I'm hit," Caleb yelled back. "But I'll live. Git the womenfolk out of that burnin' house!"

Shiloh reached the front of the house at the same time O'Brien did. The front of the house was engulfed in flames.

"The women are still inside!" O'Brien shouted over the roar of the flames.

Shiloh spurred his horse and charged around to the back porch. As he jumped down, Caleb called from beside the well.

"If they're alive, they'll be in the tunnel!"

Shiloh ran onto the back porch and looked through the glass in the back door. Three walls of the kitchen were burning, but he could see Hannah trying to drag her mother to the root cellar stairs. He pushed open the door and bolted through the flames to reach them.

"Down the stairs, Hannah" he shouted as he lifted Sarah from the floor. "Open the tunnel!"

Hannah ran down ahead of him and swung the wall of shelves away from the tunnel entrance; she grabbed the lantern she and her mother had been working by and led Shiloh into the tunnel. They ran to the far end, and Shiloh laid Sarah on the tunnel floor long enough to get the trapdoor open and clear the dirt and grass away then he boosted Hannah to the top of the ladder. Before she could start to climb, O'Brien reached in and lifted her out. Shiloh handed Sarah up to him.

"Take care of them; I'm going back to see if I can save anything!"

Shiloh ran back down the tunnel and up the stairs to the study. The fire had not yet reached that part of the house, but the room was filling with smoke. He took a deep breath, held it and moved into the room. He took the colonel's duster down from its peg and spread it on the floor, then he opened the rolltop desk and started emptying drawers and pigeonholes onto the duster. He emptied the gun rack and the cabinet beneath it, piling everything he found onto the duster. He was running out of breath, but he took a last look around. He took the framed map, a framed daguerreotype print and two framed photographs from the wall. He quickly rolled the duster around the pile, tucked it under his arm and grabbed the map with his free hand. Flames were beginning to lick their way through one wall as he went through the door. He breathed again at the bottom of the root cellar stairs and carried the things he had managed to save to the end of the tunnel. O'Brien was coming down the ladder.

"Mrs. Hadley is okay, so is Hannah, and Caleb will be."

"Help me move as much of the food as we can from the root cellar to the tunnel before the house falls in on it!" Shiloh told him as he started back down the tunnel.

They started by throwing the tinned cans as far as they could down the tunnel, with Shiloh tossing them to O'Brien, who then flung them through the entrance. They carried the sacks and barrels, running an obstacle course of strewn cans and managing to avoid twisting an ankle. They were working on the glass bottles of food Sarah and Hannah had put up from the garden harvest when pieces of the floor above began to fall between the floor joists.

"Time to retreat, General, sir," O'Brien told Shiloh, as he pulled him into the tunnel.

The two of them gathered up cans as they went and stacked them near the ladder.

"Let's take a break and check on the others," Shiloh said. "We've saved what we could."

Sarah was conscious but still woozy; she was sitting on the ground where O'Brien had brushed away the snow and leaning against the well beside Caleb, whose leg was being bandaged by Hannah.

"Hannah says you saved us from the fire," Sarah said. "Thank you very much."

"If I hadn't, Hannah would have," Shiloh told her. "She was dragging you to the stairs when I got there."

"I don't know if I could have gotten her down the stairs without breaking her to pieces," Hannah told him. "I was planning on trying to hold her head and shoulders up while I backed down and let the rest of her bounce on the stairs."

"Good plan," Shiloh said, grinning at the picture in his head. "I'd better hitch the team to the wagon; we need to get Caleb to a doctor, and I left a fellow called Swede in the cave. Apparently, George Vickers had a run-in with the marshal, and Swede caught a bullet trying to get out of the way. Is there a doctor in town?"

"There is," Caleb answered. "A youngster, but he seems to know his business."

"If George hasn't bled to death by now, we'll need to get him to the doctor, too," O'Brien said. "I shot him twice, and Hannah shot him once."

Hannah looked up at Shiloh with pleading eyes.

"He was going to shoot mother."

As tears began to roll down her cheeks, Shiloh knelt down beside her and held her to him.

"You did the right thing, Hannah," he assured her. "You saved your mother's life."

"I meant to kill him."

"He meant to kill your mother."

* * * * * * *

While Shiloh hitched the team to the wagon, Sarah and Hannah bandaged George's legs and arm, and O'Brien moved the bodies of Val and Slade to the woodshed to be buried later.

"Wasn't there somebody else?" Shiloh asked, as he and O'Brien lifted Caleb and George into the wagon.

"Slim," O'Brien said. "He swore to me that none of the hands had any idea that George meant to harm Mrs. Hadley or Hannah, said Ryan was drawing his gun to try to stop him when Hannah fired. I suggested a warmer climate and let him go."

Shiloh nodded and looked back to where the house had been. The fireplace, chimney and foundation stones were still standing; nothing else was left but a few charred timbers and burning embers. Sarah and Hannah were standing beside the wagon, arms around each other, staring at the ruins of their home. Shiloh walked over to them.

"We'll rebuild it for you," he told them.

"No, we will build another house in its place," Sarah said. "One more suited to the country."

"Whatever you want," Shiloh agreed. "O'Brien will help me and Caleb, when his leg is mended. And I think Swede is going to survive; he'll help."

"I am so grateful to all of you," Sarah told him; she turned to face the wagon and whispered. "I think George is truly insane; he meant to build an empire and make me his queen."

George was lying in the wagon, whimpering.

"George, who did you hire to shoot the J H Connected hands?" Shiloh asked.

"I didn't hire him; why would I?" he asked defiantly. "I killed Jonathan Hadley with a rock, and I shot my father. I don't need to hire someone else to do my killing."

All of them were shocked at his admission. Caleb looked up from the wagonbed.

"Then this ain't the end of it."

CHAPTER NINETEEN

By the time the wagon with three wounded men pulled to a stop outside the picket fence in front of the doctor's house, rumors were spreading like wildfire through White Sulphur Springs. A young boy had run ahead of the wagon and told the doctor they were coming, so he was waiting at the gate.

"Swede's the worst hurt, Doc," Caleb said. "Take care of him first. I'll keep, so will George."

"Would you gentlemen carry him inside, please?" The doctor asked, indicating Shiloh and O'Brien. "I don't know where I'll put him when I'm done. George has kept me busy today and filled up my beds. When he rode out of town this morning, he left two men dead, one dying and two others wounded, including Marshal Hobbs."

"How's Dan doin', Doc?" Caleb asked, as Swede was being lifted out of the wagon. "He goin' to make it?"

"It's a little early to tell, but I think he's going to be alright."

"Dr. Carson, is there anything I can do to help you?"

"Thank you for the offer, Mrs. Hadley, but my wife assists me very ably, and my surgery is a rather small room . . ."

"So I would just be in the way," Sarah finished for him.

"I wouldn't have put it that way," Carson said. "Please don't be offended."

"I am not offended, but all of these men, except for George Vickers, have risked everything to protect my daughter and me. I want them to have the best care possible."

"They will all get the best care I can give, including George," the doctor assured her.

"I understand, and I thank you, sir."

Once all the wounded men were moved into the house and out of the cold, Sarah decided to go shopping.

"I shall need a new cookstove, and it may take weeks or even months to get one shipped, so I might as well order it," she said. "We can put it in the bunkhouse until a new house can be built."

O'Brien looked up and grinned.

"Please be tellin' them to hurry it along. A poor Irish lad could suffer serious starvation in weeks or months."

"Do not worry, Mr. O'Brien," Sarah assured him. "I have cooked over open fires; I am certain I can manage to keep you alive with the pot-bellied stove in the bunkhouse until I have something better to work with."

"Aye, ma'am, I'll not be doubtin' that you can. And I'm certain sure that the fine Irishman, Michael Angelo, could have painted murals on barn walls, but the results would never have equaled the ceiling of the Sistine Chapel."

"Mr. O'Brien," Sarah told him. "I do believe you are full up to your smooth tongue with Irish blarney."

"Aye, ma'am, Tipperary born and bred."

As Sarah and Hannah left the doctor's house, Shiloh and O'Brien stayed behind to shuffle patients for the doctor. When the ladies were on the boardwalk approaching Jenkins' store, Hannah looked at her mother in puzzlement.

"Mother, I thought Michelangelo was Italian."

"He was, Hannah, and Michael O'Brien well knows it," Sarah said, chuckling and attempting to mimic O'Brien's voice.

"Then why. . .oh, I understand, that's what you meant when

you said he was full of Irish blarney. He was giving the Irish credit, as if anything worthwhile could only be accomplished by the Irish. But he doesn't truly believe that; he was only making a joke."

"That is exactly right, honey."

"Will I ever understand people as well as you do?"

"You are doing pretty well already," Sarah said, as they entered the store.

Jenkins greeted them immediately.

"Mrs. Hadley, rumors have sure been flying today. I heard a good one that your hired man, Shiloh, is still alive and a bad one that George Vickers set fire to your house. I hope the good one's true and the bad one's false."

On the way to town, it had been decided that since George would tell everyone that Shiloh was alive, there was no further point in trying to maintain the deception, so Sarah answered honestly.

"Fortunately, Shiloh *is* alive; his hair is a bit singed, and he has some burns that will probably be painful for a while. He charged through the flames to rescue us. I was unconscious, thanks to George, but Hannah was already dragging me to safety when Shiloh plunged through the flames."

"Well, that was certainly very brave, young lady," Jenkins told Hannah. "And did you really shoot George Vickers?"

"He was going to shoot Mother, Mr. Jenkins, but I'm not proud of it."

"Nevertheless, that was also very brave."

"No, sir, it was just—necessary."

Sensing Hannah's discomfort, Sarah changed the subject.

"Unfortunately, the house burned to the ground."

"How tragic," Jenkins said. "The two of you have already suffered more heartbreak than most people could bear. Will you be returning east now?"

"No, sir, the ranch is our home, the only home Hannah has ever known," Sarah said. "We will not abandon it. A new house will be built."

"I admire your courage and determination," he responded. "And I'm very glad that you and Hannah came through the ordeal without injury."

Sarah unconsciously reached up to touch her stiff, swollen neck, but she did not think that or her other bumps and bruises worth mentioning.

"I shall need some things for the new house, a cookstove for one, and some things to work with while we are all living in the bunkhouse," she said.

"I have a small cookstove in the store," Jenkins told her. "The quality is good, but it doesn't have nearly as many features as your Monarch had."

"How long will it take to get a new Monarch if I place the order today?"

"At least a month, probably several," he said.

"Then order one for me," Sarah said. "And let me look at what you have in the store; it will probably serve much better in the interim than the pot-bellied stove in the bunkhouse."

"I'm sure it will," Jenkins agreed.

As Sarah examined the cookstove, Hannah browsed through the store. She spotted a porcelain doll on a high shelf out of her reach.

"Mr. Jenkins, may I look at this doll, please?"

"Of course," he said. "I put it up high to protect it."

The shelf, well above Hannah's reach, was not even a stretch for him.

"You're very tall, aren't you?" Hannah commented.

"Six foot, six inches in my stocking feet," he said proudly. "My pa always liked to say I got my height from him and my brains from Ma."

"My father always teased Mother that I got my looks from her and my brains from him," Hannah said. "But he secretly told me once that he thought Mother was even smarter than he was, and that I was very much like her."

"Then you both must be very smart indeed," Jenkins said. "I know for a fact that your father was a very smart man."

"Thank you, Mr. Jenkins," Sarah said, as she joined them. "That is very kind of you."

"You're welcome, Mrs. Hadley. Would you like to look in the catalog now and show me exactly which cookstove you want?"

"Yes, and I think I will buy the one you have here," she said. "If there is room in the wagon, we shall pick it up when we leave town. Caleb says he is going back with us, and the doctor says he is not."

"If there's a wager in there, I'd put my money on Caleb," Jenkins told her, as he opened the catalog.

"I would have to agree."

"Mother, before you look at the stoves, would you look at this doll? Do you think it would make a good Christmas present?"

"What do you think, Hannah?"

"I think it's the most beautiful doll I have ever seen. It isn't cuddly like the doll you made me, but I guess I am getting a little too big for 'cuddly.'"

Sarah laughed.

"Honey, I hope you never get too big for 'cuddly.' I was not too big for 'cuddly' when you were born, and one day you shall have babies who will not want their mother to be too big for 'cuddly.' But it is a beautiful doll, and it might make a very nice Christmas gift."

"Thank you for letting me look at it," Hannah told Jenkins as she handed the doll back to him.

"You're very welcome."

When Sarah had picked out a cookstove and the essential items they would need for moving into the bunkhouse, she and Hannah started for the door. Then she stopped.

"Mr. Jenkins, I forgot to ask. Is there any mail for the ranch?"

"Oh, I'm sorry," he said. "I'm afraid I forgot, too, and you have several things that look important, a letter from the territorial marshal, one from the governor and a package from the Pinkerton Agency. Have you hired the Pinkertons to catch the man that's been shooting folks out your way?"

"Well, not yet," Sarah said. "But, if these two letters do not tell me that the territorial marshal is going to take immediate action, I suppose that is an option I should consider. Something has to be done to stop that assassin."

"Do you have any idea why the man is shooting folks?" Jenkins asked.

"No sir, none whatsoever."

CHAPTER TWENTY

The White Sulphur Springs jail had two cells. When Doctor Carson finished treating and bandaging George Vickers, Shiloh and O'Brien moved George into one of them and the wounded gunhand George had abandoned that morning into the other. Swede would stay in a bed next to Dan Hobbs, and, if there had been a wager, Jenkins would have won. Caleb was going back to the ranch. At the store, Jenkins relieved Smoke behind the bar long enough to have the big man help load the heavy cast iron stove. With Shiloh and O'Brien on one end and Smoke on the other, the stove was lifted into the wagon and tied securely so that it would not fall on Caleb. Then the other purchases were loaded into the wagon.

"You two given any thought to how you're goin' to get that thing into the bunkhouse by yourselves?" Caleb asked.

"Not yet," Shiloh admitted. "Have you, O'Brien?"

"We'll think of something," he said. "An Irish lad has to eat."

"Ah gits off work in 'bout an hour," Smoke offered. "Ah could ride out that way an' give y'all a hand."

"That is very generous, Smoke," Sarah said. "And you can help us eat the first meal cooked on the stove."

"That, alone, will be worth the trip," O'Brien said. "I promise."

Smoke shook hands around; when he came to Shiloh, he held on a bit longer.

"Massuh Clifton, it's been a lotta years since we last got to see each otheh. Maybe we ken do some catchin' up."

"Call me Shiloh, Smoke. You've been a free man a long time, and I never was really your master."

"Nah suh, Ah guess not, but you owned me long enough to set me free. Only man who eveh did more fo' me was Jesus when he let hisself be hung on that ol' cross."

As Smoke went back to the saloon to finish his shift, the J H Connected group started out of town.

"It's amazing how God orders a man's life," Shiloh said to no one in particular.

"Are you referring to something specific?" O'Brien asked.

"Of all the people from my past that He could have sent to meet me in the Montana Territory, I might have guessed you would be one, but I don't think I would have ever guessed that Jimbo's Tommy would be the other. Smoke is very much like Jimbo in all the important ways. And out here we can be friends, brothers in Christ, without the lingering prejudices he faced in Virginia."

"Some folks brung them lingerin' prejudices west when they come," Caleb reminded him.

"That's true," Shiloh admitted. "But we can help see that it remains the exception out here rather than the commonplace."

"We can try," Caleb offered.

When they reached the ranch, Sarah felt strange driving the team to the bunkhouse, but she never let it show. As Shiloh and O'Brien were moving him inside, Caleb insisted he be put on one of the bunks near the pot-bellied stove.

"Shiloh has already given us the foreman's room," Sarah reminded him.

"You'll need more room than that," Caleb said. "An' while I'm stove up, I'd get cabin fever in there all winter by myself."

"All right, gentlemen," Sarah agreed. "Put him in a bunk out here, and thank you, Caleb."

While they were waiting for Smoke to arrive, Shiloh and O'Brien took the wagon up to the end of the tunnel and loaded everything they had saved from the fire. As they were coming back down, they saw Hannah skipping toward the bunkhouse with something in her hand, but neither could make out what. When they reached the bunkhouse, Hannah showed them her prize.

"I was digging in the ashes where the back porch was, and just look what I found, the triangle and its clanger!"

"I'll clean it up and hang it before supper," O'Brien promised.

"Oh, thank you so much!"

"He may be doing it for himself as much as for you," Shiloh teased.

"Oh, don't be mean," Hannah scolded. "I'll have fun ringing it again," she said happily then sadness swept across her face. "I'll miss the piano most of all."

"We shall find you another," Sarah told her. "I have asked Mr. Jenkins to see if he can find a good one closer than St. Louis."

Shiloh reached into the wagon and pulled out the rolled-up duster with the items he had retrieved from the study.

"I'll carry this inside for you, the rifles and cartridges make it pretty heavy, but you'll want to go through it. I emptied out the desk, thinking you might have deeds and other important papers there. I also managed to save the map of the ranch and the pictures that were hanging above the desk."

When Sarah saw the daguerreotype and the two photographs, tears filled her eyes.

"Oh, Hannah, look!" she cried. "These are irreplaceable," she told Shiloh. "I promised Hannah they would one day be hers, and I thought we had lost them."

Sarah handed them to Hannah one at a time; Hannah knew them well. The daguerreotype was of Jonathan Hadley in his military uniform; one of the photographs was a wedding picture of her mother and father, and the other was a family portrait with Sarah holding Hannah when she was a few months old and a proud Jonathan looking lovingly at his daughter. Hannah looked at each one then stacked them together and set them aside. She put her arms around Shiloh and squeezed tightly.

"I've been afraid that I would forget what Father looked like, she said. "Sometimes, I can't quite picture him in my mind. With these safe, I will always be able to remind myself of what he looked like and how much he loved me. Thank you for saving them."

CHAPTER TWENTY-0NE

When Smoke rode up toward dusk, Hannah stared at his horse in disbelief; the horse was large enough to make the huge man seem small.

"What kind of horse is that?" she asked.

"A Clydesdale," Smoke told her. "Most folks don' use 'em fo' ridin', they pulls heavy wagons an' plows an' things wif 'em. Ah uses him to plow mah garden an' pull mah wagon, too. Ah calls him Samson, 'cuz he's so strong an' hairy."

Hannah giggled at that.

"Must have had that saddle special made," Shiloh said.

"Yes, suh, Ah bought Samson from a Quaker man in Pennsylvania an' rode him barebacked to Missouri. When Ah rode into St. Joe, a man stopped me in the street an' says, 'Ah ken make a saddle to fit both you an' that horse,' so Ah let him."

"Where do you keep him?" Hannah asked. "I would remember if I had seen him in town."

"Theah's a little barn an' corral behind the store an' saloon wheah Mr. Jenkins keeps his horse; he lets me put Samson in theah when Ah rides him to work. An' Ah built a place fo' him next to mah cabin."

"Where is your cabin?" Sarah asked.

"A little ways west of town on the north fork of the Smith Riveh'," Smoke said. "That's why Frank Vickers didn' have no use fo' me, Ah filed a homestead on 160 acres along the riveh' on land he figured wuz Slash V range, but he didn't have no deed or patent—next year, Ah will. Then Ah'm gonna git married."

"Do you have someone picked out yet?" Hannah asked.

"Yes, Miss Hannah, Jenny an' me been sweethearts since we wuz young'uns. She's been workin' fo' a family in Richmond an' savin' her money 'til Ah ken send fo' her."

"Did you sell the parcel you were farming next to your Daddy?" Shiloh asked.

"Nah, suh, that land you give to me Ah give to Daisy an' her husband fo' a weddin' present," Smoke said. "That way they'll be close by to look after Momma an' Daddy as they git old. Lotta things has changed back theah, but some things is changin' too slow fo' me. Ah didn't know whut Ah wuz lookin' fo' when Ah left Virginny; the Good Lord showed it to me when Ah got heah."

"What are you growing on your 160 acres?" Shiloh asked.

"Right now, besides the garden, Ah'm raisin' chickens an' hogs. Ah sells most of the eggs an' meat to the hotel restaurant. An' Ah'm buildin' a herd of Jersey cows to sell milk; Frank Vickers didn' like that none neither, 'cuz Ah grazes 'em on open range durin' the day then herds 'em back inside mah fence at night, so none of the longhorn bulls gets to mah cows."

"You do all that and work full time for Mr. Jenkins?" Sarah asked.

"Not all by mahself," Smoke said. "Ah took in a orphan boy a few years back; he reminds me of yo' Dan'l, Massuh Clif—Shiloh, an' he earns his keep by helpin' me. He's thirteen now an' does the feedin' an' milkin' when Ah's workin' in the saloon or sto', but mostly now his job is to keep mah milk cows on fresh grass durin' the day an' chase the longhorn bulls away from 'em. Ah've got a couple of Jersey bulls fo' breedin', an' Ah don't want no mixed-breed calves."

"What is the boy's name?" Hannah asked. "And why haven't we seen him at church with you?"

"Well, his given name is Oscar," Smoke told her. "But he didn't like it none too well, so Ah started callin' him Cotton 'cuz his hair wuz 'bout like cotton in the sun when he first come to me. His hair's turnin' darker now, Miss Hannah, 'bout the color of yo' hair. An' we takes turns goin' to church so one of us is always home to keep an eye on the place."

"Why, I know who Cotton is," Hannah said. "He's really nice, and he sings beautifully. Mrs. Reardon frequently asks him to sing solo parts in church. But I had no idea you were raising him."

"Ah was afraid folks might not like the idea of me raisin' a white boy, so we neveh tol' nobody but the preacher an' his wife. Frank Vickers knew, an' George an' some of the Slash V hands know, but Frank musta tol' his folks to leave us be, 'cause Ah ain't had no trouble from 'em since Cotton showed up at mah cabin door one rainy night, lookin' fo' a meal an' a dry place to sleep."

"I've seen the lad out on the range herding those Jersey cows," O'Brien said. "But I had no idea they were yours. Only thing I ever heard Frank say about the cows or fences was that the cows had a right to be on open range, that one day all the ranches would end up fenced like farms back east, and he hoped he wouldn't live to see that day."

"Ah guess maybe Mr. Frank wuz a better man an' a wiser one than Ah knowed," Smoke said. "Ah never had no doubts 'bout him bein' an honest man."

"Smoke, does Jenny know about Cotton?" Shiloh asked.

"Ah tol' her in the first letter Ah wrote after he decided to stay on an' help me. Now she puts a letter to him in wif her letters to me, an' he puts one to her in wif the letters Ah write. Ah think he's as anxious fo' me to be able to send fo' her as Ah am."

"Did you teach him to read an' write?" Caleb asked.

"He already had a pretty good start when he come to me," Smoke said. "But Ah've tried to make sure he gets schoolin'. The preacher an' his wife have helped me get books fo' him, an' they's helped me with the teachin'. But Cotton's smart enough to get most of it on his own, an' now he's teachin' me 'bout things Ah neveh had no chance to learn. Right now he's mostly interested in readin' 'bout hist'ry an' gov'ment an' law; if'n you see him out on the range, you'll likely see him wif a book restin' on his saddle horn."

"Sounds like you've done a good job with him," Caleb said.

"Ah've tried to do right by him," Smoke said. "The Good Lord knowed we needed each otheh when He sent the boy to mah cabin. Ah wuz plannin' to help him set up a homestead of his own when he come of age, an' Ah will if'n that's whut he wants, but lately Ah've been thinkin' maybe the Lord is gonna want him to go back east to college. If'n that's His plan, Ah reckon He'll open doors Ah cain't when the time comes."

"When the time comes, Smoke," Sarah said. "Maybe God will use us to help open those doors. Jonathan's parents are good Christian people, and they have some influence. Please feel as free to ask for our help as you have been willing to offer your help to us."

"Ah will, Miz Hadley, an' Ah thanks you."

"Anybody besides me think it would be a good idea to unload that new cookstove?" O'Brien asked.

"Mr. O'Brien, how could you possibly be hungry so soon?" Hannah asked. "I am certain we fed you yesterday or the day before. Surely, you don't think you need to eat every day."

"Miss Hannah, not only do I think I need to eat every day, but several times every day. And while you and your mother fed me a wonderful breakfast before all the excitement began this morning, I was only able to manage a small sandwich while we were in town, just one side of beef between two loaves of bread, so I'm truly famished now, and, if we don't unload the stove soon, I'll be too weak to help."

"Mr. O'Brien, I must have been mistaken when I assumed

184

blarney to be green like the grass of your Emerald Isle," Hannah told him. "I am certain now that the blarney has risen above your smooth tongue, filled your head completely and given your eyes their brilliant blue color."

That brought laughs and chuckles from everyone, including O'Brien.

"You're too kind to flatter me so," he said. "Your mother has done well to teach you to respect your elders, but, if she doesn't mind, would you drop the 'Mr.?' It makes me feel old, and we're friends now, family really, so perhaps you could call me Michael, darlin'."

After a nod from Sarah, Hannah gave him a sweet smile.

"Very well, from now on, I shall call you Michael Darlin'."

"'Pears to me," Caleb said. "That Irish blarney is as catchin' as cholera and spreadin' like wildfire on the J H Connected. Michael Darlin', you might want to ask Miz Hadley where she wants that cookstove before you unload it. No sense havin' to move it twice."

"Actually," Sarah said. "I have not given any thought to where it should go."

"May I make a suggestion?" Shiloh asked.

"Certainly," Sarah assured him. "I would appreciate your advice."

"Well, the cookstove uses the same size stovepipe as the pot-bellied stove. If we put it there, it'll be close to your rooms. We can build shelves and put up pegs for supplies and utensils along the walls. We can move the pot-bellied stove to the far end of the bunkhouse, and tomorrow I can make a hole in the roof for a new stovepipe. If we move some of these extra bunks out of the way, I could put up a temporary partition between the stove and our bunks and move the table and chairs to put in the space between the partition and your rooms. That would provide you and Hannah a bit more privacy and more working room to make do with until we can build the new house."

"That should work very well," Sarah agreed. "I bought some

new lanterns; one can hang over the table, and some of the others can be hung on the walls or from the ceiling near the cookstove and shelves. And it is a long way to the well pump from here; perhaps, I could have a water barrel as well."

"If we put two on a stand, you can use one until it's empty then use the other until one of us can get a chance to refill the first. If each has a spigot, you won't have to bother with a dipper."

"And with the barrels on a stand, Hannah and I will not have to break our backs bending over the barrels; we can just hold our pots under the spigots. That is very thoughtful of you."

"Trust a lazy man to find easy ways to do things," Shiloh said.

"I would say you have as much laziness about you as Caleb does, exactly none."

* * * * * *

After the cookstove was in place and while Sarah and Hannah were cooking the evening meal, Shiloh, O'Brien and Smoke went to the burned-out ruins of the ranch house. In the failing light at the end of day, they examined the fireplace and chimney and looked carefully at the foundation stones.

"I think the fireplace and chimney are sound," O'Brien said. "It'll take a bit of work to clean up the stones, but other than that I don't see any problems. Some of the foundation stones are going to have to be reset or replaced."

"And one of the root cellar walls will need repair," Shiloh said. "Looks like the cookstove collapsed it when it fell through the floor."

"You ken lift the cookstove out uh that hole wif a block an' tackle," Smoke said. "If'n there ain't one on the ranch, Ah got one an' some heavy rope you's welcome to use. If'n you build a timber frame oveh the cellar you ken lift the stove high enough to slide some more timbers under it, angled from the floor to the top of the cellar wall, lower the stove long enough to move yo' frame to the side an' skid the stove up the timbers 'til it's out uh the hole. Then you ken back a wagon under the stove an' haul it out uh the way."

"If we build that frame tall enough, we can also use it to lift wall logs, joists and rafters into place," Shiloh said. "I don't know if there's a block and tackle on the ranch; I'll have to ask Caleb."

"When you get that stove on the wagon, Ah'd like to take a look at it," Smoke said. "Ah ken see some sheet metal damage, but if'n the cast iron pieces ain't broke, Ah might be able to fix it. Ah do mah cookin' in the fireplace, but Ah figures on addin' to the cabin, so Jenny ken have a kitchen wif a cookstove. An' that'd be a real nice stove if'n Ah ken fix it an' put some fresh stove black on it."

Before it was too dark to see, Shiloh stepped off distances to locate the fireplace and root cellar within the foundation perimeter then the three men returned to the bunkhouse.

"Caleb?" Shiloh asked. "Is there a block and tackle on the ranch?"

"Not that I know of."

"Then we'll need to borrow yours, Smoke," Shiloh said. "Would you be interested in trading some labor? You help us build a new house for the Hadleys, and I'll help you add to your cabin."

"Ah done figured on helpin' build the Hadleys a new house," Smoke told him. "But Ah'd sho' be glad fo' yo' help on mah cabin."

"You can count on my help, too," O'Brien said.

"An' mine," Caleb added. "If you wait 'til I can git out of this bed."

"We shall all help," Sarah said. "That is what neighbors are for."

"Well, that's real nice of all uh y'all; Ah appreciates it."

"And we appreciate you, Smoke," Hannah said.

CHAPTER TWENTY-TWO

Shiloh sat on his bunk, and, using a book for a desk, he wrote down the measurements he had taken then began drawing out lines for a new house. He had several arrangements to show to Sarah by the time food was on the table.

"Somebody help me up, an' I'll eat at the table," Caleb said.

"No, sir!" Hannah told him sternly. "The only reason Dr. Carson let you come home is because I promised to help nurse you, and I gave him my solemn word you would stay in bed and off that leg for two weeks." She gave him one of those smiles he cherished so much. "Are you going to make a liar out of me?"

"Nope, that I'm not goin' to do," he said. "Would it be makin' a liar out of you, if I wuz to sit up an' put my right foot on the floor while I eat? That'd help me balance."

"So long as that injured leg stays on the bed," Hannah agreed.

"Miz Hadley, yore daughter has considerable steel in her backbone," Caleb said.

"She inherited that from her father," Sarah said.

"An' I reckon you're only 'bout half right; 'pears to me she got the other half from her mother."

Sarah accepted the compliment by handing him a plate of food.

"Wait!" O'Brien said anxiously. "Hannah, aren't you

forgetting something?"

"Is it my turn to say grace?"

"Well, now that may be, and that's certainly important. But isn't it your job to let the hands know when it's time to eat?"

Hannah grabbed a lantern and dashed out the door; they all heard her gleeful shriek, followed immediately by the clanging of the triangle. O'Brien had kept his word.

* * * * * *

After supper, Sarah invited Smoke to stay the night rather than make the long ride in the dark.

"Will Cotton be worried?" Hannah asked.

"No, Missy," Smoke assured her. "Ah give a boy from town two bits to ride out an' tell Cotton that Ah wuz comin' heah an' might camp on the trail back if'n it got late."

"Smoke, there are plenty of empty bunks," Shiloh said. "If you push a couple of them together end-to-end and pad the frame ends with a blanket, you'll probably sleep a lot more comfortably than with half your legs sticking off the end exposed to the cold night air."

"Thanks, Mas—Shiloh, eveh since Ah wuz fully-growed Ah've had to make mahself a extra big bed to sleep on. When Ah settled out heah, Ah had a lady in town sew me a feather tick fo' the bed Ah built. She made it half ag'in as wide an' long as most, an' twice as thick—used enough feathers to fill up six normal-sized feather ticks. But Ah sho' sleeps good on it, an' it's big enough there'll be room fo' Jenny when we's married."

"How long 'til you've proved-up on yore homestead claim?" Caleb asked.

"In the spring, then Ah ken send fo' Jenny."

"If you're that close, why wait?" O'Brien asked.

"Ah wants Jenny to see the place fo' the first time when the grass is green an' the streams is runnin' an' the wildflowers is bloomin'. Ah wants her to grow to love the place enough to tolerate the cold, in case she's like you an' finds she don't like it much."

"That is very wise, Smoke," Sarah said.

"Ah loves it out heah," Smoke said. "Ah wants mah Jenny to love it just as much. We ken have a good life heah, if'n she's happy."

"She'll have you, Smoke," Hannah said. "She'll be happy."

"Ah prays ever' day that she is; eveh'thin' Ah builds, Ah builds fo' her."

Shiloh picked up the papers he had been working on at his bunk.

"Mrs. Hadley, if you want to look at these, I've sketched out some of the ideas Michael, Smoke and I came up with for using the existing foundation and fireplace. You can tell us what you like and don't like."

"Well, I do want to look at them," Sarah said. "But, first, I need to help Hannah with the dishes, so she can get to bed."

"Michael Darlin' will help Miss Hannah with the dishes," O'Brien said. "You go on and have a look at those sketches."

"Ah'll help, too," Smoke said.

"Okay," O'Brien agreed. "I'll wash; you dry, and Hannah can ramrod this shindig."

"I'll catch the wet dishes you drop and put the dry ones away when Smoke hands them to me." Hannah said with a grin.

"Well," Sarah said. "I guess my time is free after all. Thank you, gentlemen."

Smoke flashed Sarah an enormous grin, swept an imaginary top-hat from his head and bowed deeply from the waist. When he straightened up, his eyes were glistening, and he was very serious.

"Nobody eveh called me a gentleman befo'."

"You are very much a gentleman, Smoke," Sarah said. "In the very best sense of the word."

"Thank you, ma'am."

Sarah and Shiloh sat on the bunk next to Caleb's, so he could look at the sketches and they could get his suggestions. After carefully considering the various arrangements and suggestions, Sarah held out one of the sketches.

"I think I like this arrangement best. And I love the idea of a pump in the kitchen."

"That was Smoke's idea," Shiloh told her. "He ran a pipe from his well, so Jenny won't have to 'tote heavy buckets of water.'"

"She will appreciate that as much as Hannah and I will," Sarah said. "Do you have any idea how long it will take to build this first section?" she asked, pointing to the sketch.

"It depends on how much more good weather we have in the weeks ahead," Shiloh said. "And how soon we can stop the sharpshooter."

"Oh, dear," Sarah said as she stood up suddenly. "Shiloh, I picked up two letters and a package in town today and completely forgot about them. The package is from the Pinkerton Agency."

When she had found the mail among the supplies she did not yet have a place to put away, she returned to the bunk, sat down and handed the package to Shiloh.

"See what is in this while I find out how the territorial governor and his marshal plan to help."

"Don't you mean *if* they plan to help?" Caleb asked.

"I hope not," she said, as she ripped open the marshal's letter first. "Well, the marshal plans to be here the first week of November, as soon as he clears up 'a pressing matter in Helena'. . .apologizes for not coming sooner. . .Montana is a big territory and he has few deputies. . ." She tore into the governor's letter. "The governor has instructed the marshal to make our problem his number one priority; the rest of the letter is just more of the same self-serving political drivel the marshal wrote."

Shiloh looked up from the papers he was going through and handed her a photograph he had set aside.

"Recognize anyone?" he asked.

Sarah studied the photo carefully for several minutes, finally standing up to hold it closer to the lantern hanging above them.

"Why, this looks like. . ." She stopped and handed the picture to Caleb. "Have a look and tell us what you think."

"Could you hold that lantern down here closer?" he asked.

Sarah unhooked it and held it for him then waited as Caleb looked at each face in the picture.

"If you added a few years, a few pounds, a mustache and slightly longer sideburns to this sergeant, you'd have our storekeeper, Jenkins."

Sarah and Shiloh nodded in agreement. Sarah hung the lantern back on its hook and sat down.

"The list of names on the back identifies him as Sergeant Peter Walker. According to this," Shiloh said, holding up a paper from the package. "On the day Sgt. Walker, formerly one of Berdan's sharpshooters, was mustered out of the Union army in his home State of Illinois, the paymaster's office on the fort was robbed of more than ten thousand dollars. Walker was a suspect but has never been questioned, because he vanished off the face of the earth."

"So he moved west using a new name, changed his appearance slightly and eventually used the money to start his store and saloon in White Sulphur Springs," Sarah speculated. "What does he hope to gain by running us off of this ranch?"

"Several years ago, the Northern Pacific made plans to build a railroad across the J H Connected to reach the miners on the east slopes of the Big Belt Mountains. Jenkins must have learned of the plan, probably from the survey crew the railroad sent," Shiloh said. "What Jenkins apparently doesn't know is that the plans were abandoned shortly after the survey crew returned east."

"So he's been killin' folks an' never had no hope fer gain?" Caleb asked.

"Seems so."

"How tragic," Sarah said. "Three good men murdered for no

reason, and you could have been the fourth, Shiloh, but for the grace of God. What do we do now?"

"I'll ride into town tomorrow with Smoke and see if Dan Hobbs is well enough to deputize me so that I can arrest Jenkins."

"If he ain't?" Caleb asked.

"Who's the mayor?" Shiloh asked after a moment of thought. "If Hobbs is incapacitated, the mayor can appoint me temporarily to the marshal's job."

"Milt Green, the barber, is the mayor," Sarah said. "Do you know him?"

"No."

"Then I had better ride in to vouch for you," Sarah said. "Mr. Green is always reluctant to accept strangers at first."

"If you don't mind, I'd prefer that you remain at the ranch until this is over. I can ask Dr. Carson to recommend me."

"Very well," Sarah agreed. "But please do not take any unnecessary risks. We do not want to lose you."

"Amen to that," Caleb added.

CHAPTER TWENTY-THREE

Shiloh and Smoke were in the saddle shortly after breakfast; they rode carefully and quietly, watching for and trying to avoid places where the sharpshooter might get a shot at them. As they were getting close to town, Smoke began to voice his thoughts and questions.

"If'n Jenkins gets hung fo' murder, whut do you reckon will happen to his sto'?"

"I don't know, Smoke. If he has any family he cares about, he might leave it for them. I suppose the government might seize it, since it was probably built with part of that stolen Army payroll."

"Reckon they's any way Ah could buy it?"

"Maybe," Shiloh said. "You think you can keep up with running the store, the saloon and your farm?"

"Well, Ah ain't got no plans fo' runnin' no saloon, but, if'n Ah could buy the buildin' an' the stock in the sto', Ah could turn the saloon into a part of the sto', add a butcher shop, sell mah milk an' eggs, maybe butter an' cheese an' garden vegetables. But Ah couldn' do it by mahself. Ah'd have to get mah whole family out heah, Momma an' Daddy, mah brothers an' sisters, they wives an' husbands. Momma an' Daddy could live in the back of the sto' an' run it wif the help of us young'uns. An' Ah could help mah

195

brothers an' sisters to get started on farms of they own. Ah wouldn' raise no beef cows, but Ah could buy beef from Miz Hadley. An' mah family would all be togetheh, maybe even some of Jenny's folks would want to come."

"Sounds like a good plan," Shiloh said. "I don't see any reason why it wouldn't work. You think your whole family would come west?"

"If'n Momma an' Daddy thinks it's a good idea an' come, the rest will come."

"How hard will it be to convince them?"

"Is you plannin' to stay heahabouts?" Smoke asked.

"I don't know, Smoke. Why?"

"'Cuz if'n Ah writes Momma an' Daddy an' tells 'em you's goin' to be mah neighbor, Ah don' think nuthin' could stop 'em from comin'."

"I doubt that."

"Ah don'," Smoke said. "An' it ain't none of mah business, but Ah thinks you should stay heah an' marry Miz Hadley."

"Why would she want to marry me?" Shiloh asked.

"'Cuz you's the finest man Ah've eveh knowed, an' you can make sure she don' lose her home. But mostly 'cuz she an' Miss Hannah both love you, an' you love them. An' you an' Miz Hadley may be the only two people in this part of the country who don' know it. Theah, Ah've said mah piece; now Ah'll stop meddlin' in yo' business."

"Do you really think Sarah Hadley loves me?"

"Yes, suh," Smoke told him. "But Ah also thinks she's the kind of lady who won't say nuthin' 'bout her feelin's unless you tell her you love her an' ask her if'n she feels the same way. Ah reckon that won' be none too easy fo' you, but if'n you ain't willin' to risk her sayin' no, Ah don' thinks you'll eveh know how much she wants to say yes."

* * * * * * *

When they reached the doctor's house, Shiloh pulled the Pinkerton Agency package out of his saddlebags and led Smoke inside.

"How's the Swede doing, Dr. Carson?" Shiloh asked.

"Very well, I may let you take him home next week."

"Is Marshal Hobbs in good enough shape to talk to me?"

"May I ask the nature of your business? If this is a social call, I'd prefer to have you come back in a few days."

"I need to get him to deputize me, so I can arrest a murderer."

"You know who's shooting the J H Connected hands?"

Shiloh nodded.

"Smoke, would you mind waiting for Shiloh out here? The Swede is sleeping, and it would be better if we can keep the disturbance to a minimum."

"Ah needs the marshal to make me a deputy, too. Ah's stickin' wif Shiloh 'til this is oveh."

"Then both of you follow me."

Dan Hobbs was awake when they entered the room.

"Please try to be as quiet as you can," Dr. Carson told them before he turned to go.

"Hello, ghost," the marshal said when he saw Shiloh. "I'm pretty sure I went to your funeral."

"Sorry to disappoint you," Shiloh said with a grin. "But I think the deception served its purpose."

Shiloh showed Hobbs the photograph and let him find the man they knew as Jenkins on his own then he told him briefly of the payroll robbery and of Jenkins' service as a Union army sharpshooter.

"Well," Hobbs said, holding up the picture. "This is enough to arrest him for the payroll theft, an' you can search the store, saloon an' his barn for the Army payroll. If you happen to find a Whitworth rifle while you're searching, he'll likely get hung for murder. I'll swear you in here, an' you can stop by my office an' pick up a couple of deputy badges. Joe Turner is watchin' my prisoners; he knows where the badges are."

After Shiloh and Smoke were sworn in as deputies, they started to leave.

"Try not to get yourselves shot," Hobbs called after them. "The Doc is plumb wore out from all the business he's been gettin' from my office."

Shiloh paused in the door.

"What happened that started all the shooting when you went to arrest George?"

"Judgment error on my part. I figured a sawed-off shotgun would keep things civilized; didn't expect no resistance from cowboys an' didn't know that bunch with George thought they was fightin' men. One of 'em went for his gun an' got himself an' two others killed. I emptied both barrels of the shotgun. While I was drawin' my handgun, George put a couple of bullets in me, then I guess he lost interest in me. He started shootin' at Swede then jumped on his horse an' took out after him. I fired several shots at him, but I was in pretty bad shape for shootin' along about then. I doubt that I even managed to hit the livery barn behind him."

"Have you been awake enough to find out from Swede or Dr. Carson what happened at the J H Connected?"

"Yeah, I reckon George must have gone back to the Slash V an' picked up some more of his gunhands," Hobbs said. "I wonder if George even told them what happened in town?"

"He'll probably tell you when you ask him," Shiloh said. "He wasn't bashful when he admitted killing both Jonathan Hadley and his father."

"Well, he's bashful now; he's got a lawyer tellin' him to keep his mouth shut."

"What's going on out at the Slash V?"

"Gunhands are gone; the lawyer's seein' to it that the cowhands are workin' an' gettin' paid—at least through the winter."

"That's good," Shiloh said. "I guess we'd better get some badges and round up Jenkins. You've only get two cells. Who do you want us to put him in with?"

"If that gunhand of George's is fit to travel, tell him he's free to go if he'll promise to leave the territory. If he ain't, move him to the hotel and tell him to light a shuck when he can. He just caught some buckshot 'cause he was in the wrong place at the wrong time; I don't remember that he ever even tried to pull his gun."

"Okay, we'll stop back by when this is over. If you're asleep, we'll leave word with the doctor."

"Don't underestimate Jenkins," the marshal cautioned.

"We won't."

* * * * * * *

Shiloh and Smoke stopped in at the marshal's office for the deputy badges. While they were there, Shiloh took down two sawed-off shotguns from the wall rack and found a box of buckshot in a desk drawer.

"You know how to use one of these?" Shiloh asked Smoke.

"Ah never used one wif the barrels cut off," Smoke said. "But Ah've hunted wif a double-barreled shotgun mo'n once."

"The shot spreads sooner, and you need to be closer to hit anything, but loading, shooting and reloading is the same."

As the two men walked side-by-side up the boardwalk toward the store, Shiloh told Smoke how he planned to try to handle the situation.

"Do you usually go in the front or the back when you go in to work at the saloon or the store?" he asked.

"Well', if'n Ah'm comin' from home, Ah puts Samson in the barn out back an' comes in the back way. If'n Ah'm comin' from someplace in town, Ah uses the front door."

"How about going in the back way today?" Shiloh asked. "If I go in alone I may be able to catch him by surprise and take him without resistance. If you go in the back way, we'll have him outflanked, and you can stop him if he tries to run out the back door. I don't know if he has any idea that we're on to him, but he saw the package from the Pinkerton Agency, so he may err on the side of caution, which, for him, may mean shoot first and run fast. And he won't be depending on the long-range rifle; he'll most likely have a handgun or a shotgun—maybe both. He may even be one of those folks who favors a knife. So don't take any chances until you know he's been disarmed."

"You wants me to make mahself busy wif somethin' out back 'til Ah hears you talkin' to him?" Smoke asked.

"That's a good idea," Shiloh said. "I won't show the badge or the shotgun until I'm pretty close; from there things may or may not go as planned."

"Okay, give me a couple of minutes to gets around back."

When Smoke turned the back corner of the building, he waved to let Shiloh know he was ready. But when Shiloh reached the front door, he found it locked. Before he had decided what to do next, he heard Smoke unlocking it from the inside.

"He's done gone," Smoke told him. "Safe's empty; cash drawer is open, so Ah reckon it's empty, too. An' we'll prob'ly find his horse gone. Ah didn' look when Ah saw the sto' wuz locked an' empty."

"How did you get in? Do you have your own key?" Shiloh asked.

"Uh huh, Jenkins decided Ah needed a key three or fo' years ago."

"Well, let's search the store and the saloon, then we can take these badges and shotguns back to the jail."

"You just gonna let him go?" Smoke asked.

"No, but the badges are only good to the edge of town, and the marshal might want to keep the scatterguns; especially, since I didn't ask his permission to use them. No, I'm going to have to try to track Jenkins from town. Once I have an idea where he's headed, I may go back to the ranch and pick up a few things, or I may just get what I need from the store and leave an I.O.U. I wonder if he left during the night, or if he opened the store this morning and left when we rode into town together."

"Ah don' know," Smoke said. "But Jake's tendin' bar; he'll know if'n the sto's been open. First person that couldn' get in would've gone next door to ask, even if'n it wuz a woman who wouldn' go into the saloon, she would've asked somebody sittin' on one of the benches out front or called in to someone inside. So Jake'll know whether the sto's been open at all this mornin' or pretty close to when it closed up."

"Okay, let's look in Jenkins' quarters first," Shiloh said. "If he left during the night, there probably won't be anything to find. If he left in a hurry this morning he might have overlooked something that would give me an idea where he's headed."

"Is you aimin' to go after him by yo'self?"

"Don't see that I have a choice," Shiloh said. "You've got a farm to take care of, and, with Caleb and Swede out of action, I can't take O'Brien. I don't know of anyone else I'd trust, and most folks would just be in the way."

"Cotton ken take care of the farm by hisself fo' as long as this takes. An' Ah ken help you catch this man, Shiloh," Smoke told him. "Ah'm good in the woods. Yo' Dan'l always told folks Ah wuz a shadow in the woods. Ah'm bigger now, but mah eyes an' ears is just as sharp as they wuz then, an' Ah ain't forgot how to git along. These evehgreen forests gives a man mo' cover than bare oak trees in winter, an' the soft needles under 'em don't crunch like dry oak leaves. Ah ken move a lot faster wifout makin' no noise, if'n Ah needs to."

"Jenkins has already killed three men that we know of," Shiloh said. "And you make a mighty big target. You sure you want to come with me?"

"The Good Book says a man ain't got no greater love than that he lays down his life fo' a friend. Jesus done did that fo' both of us, an' we's gonna spend eternity together; whether it's on this earth or in heaven don' really matter. When Ah left Virginny, Ah didn' neveh expect to see you ag'in, but Jenkins has got to be stopped. If'n the Good Lord still has a purpose fo' us beyond catchin' him, He'll keep us safe, an' if'n one of us is called home helpin' the Hadleys, then we'll all be together in the heahafter. If'n you left wifout me, Ah'd just foller you at a distance."

Shiloh reached out and shook Smoke's hand.

"Then let's get busy."

It did not take long to go through Jenkins quarters in the back of the store, and the two men learned only that Jenkins appeared to have left most everything behind.

"He's traveling light," Shiloh said. "Don't see how he could be thinking that there is any hope for his original plan to still work; maybe he wants to get some miles behind him and try to outdistance any pursuit."

"He might just want us to think that," Smoke suggested. "If'n he's got him a hidey-hole, he might try to lose us while tryin' to make it look like he's headed clean out uh the territory, then he could circle back an' hole up fo' the winter. Ah tracked a deer once that led me in a big circle to his own backtrail. Looked to me like he wuz prob'ly watchin' from the trees as I follered his tracks on the ground then he took off in the opposite direction once I wuz past him. One thing Ah ken tell you 'bout Jenkins, he thinks ahead, an' he's a smart man, smarter'n that deer was. Whateveh he's gonna do, he's got it all planned out; our best bet fo' catchin' him is to put enough pressure on him to spoil his plannin' an' force him to react to what we's doin'. If'n we ken do that, he might make a mistake that'll give us a chance to catch him."

"Did you ever catch up with that deer?" Shiloh asked.

"Nah, suh, but Ah learned not to let that trick work on me a second time."

In the saloon they learned that Jenkins had opened the store at the normal time that morning.

"Did he say where he wuz goin' or when he might be back?" Smoke asked.

"Didn't say nuthin' a'tall," Jake told him. "I never knew he'd closed up until the preacher's wife called me to the door an' asked me when the store would be open ag'in."

"When wuz that?" Shiloh asked.

"Hour an' a half, maybe two hours ago."

"Thanks, Jake," Smoke said. "Ah'm gonna be gone fo' a while; Ah'm goin' wif Shiloh to catch up wif Jenkins. Ah reckon you an' Carl will have to relieve each other if'n you's gonna keep the saloon open. Ah'd leave the sto' locked up if Ah wuz you, leastwise 'til we find out how this is gonna turn out."

"What's this all about?" Jake asked. "Where'd Jenkins take off to?"

"We aims to find out wheah he took off to." Smoke said. "Seems Jenkins is the sharpshooter that's been killin' folks out at the J H Connected."

CHAPTER TWENTY-FOUR

Shiloh and Smoke were able to pick up Jenkins' trail from the barn where he kept his horse; it led straight north out of town.

"He doesn't seem to be trying to cover his tracks at this point," Shiloh said. "So you could be right about him leading us in the direction he wants us to think he's going. We'd lose a whole day for me to go back to the J H Connected for supplies and my packhorse, and the packhorse would slow us down some. Let's go back to the store and gather up what we need in the way of food and ammunition—do you have a rifle or any kind of handgun?"

"Ah've got a Remington revolver in my saddlebags," Smoke told him. "Mah huntin' rifle is in mah cabin. Ah quit carryin' it a while back—the scabbard kept rubbin' a raw place on Samson, an' we ain't had no trouble wif Injuns since Ah been out heah."

"Well, let's get you a rifle out of the store then."

In the store, Smoke found a new big-bore Winchester rifle just like Shiloh's, and they took all of the 45-75 WCF cartridges they found on the shelf, two hundred rounds.

"Jenkins must have gotten a new shipment," Shiloh said. "I bought him out when I first came to town."

"How many boxes do you want fo' the revolvers?" Smoke asked.

"One box apiece should be enough," Shiloh said. "We don't want to carry too much weight, and the rifles will be our primary weapons."

The two of them gathered everything they thought they needed, including a couple of extra canteens, and made a pile on the store counter. Then they divided the pile and packed their saddlebags with everything they would hold before wrapping the remainder of supplies into a pair of bundles to tie onto their saddles.

"I'll stick this I.O.U. in the empty cash drawer and settle up with whoever ends up with the store," Shiloh said.

"If'n that's me, won' be nuthin' to settle," Smoke told him.

They rode out of town following a plain trail due north. An hour before dark, they stopped, built a fire and cooked their evening meal. Then they moved on, looking for a protected place to spend the night. When they found a place, they rode on until dark and circled back to make camp. They had already discussed the need for a cold camp, so they unsaddled the horses and set about spreading their bedrolls.

"If we lay our beds out next to each other, we'll probably sleep warmer, and back-to-back we can cover the approaches to the camp," Shiloh suggested. "Probably be a good idea to take turns sleeping."

"You reckon we's gained any distance on him?"

"I doubt it; we're still on Slash V range. I'd guess he's either headed for the Little Belt Mountains to that 'hidey-hole' you suggested or around them to Fort Benton in hopes of catching a late season riverboat to get clear out of the territory. If he plans to hole up in the mountains for the winter, we can expect some kind of trick to lose us tomorrow. If he's headed for the Fort, we may see the trick, but he'll still be trying to cover a lot of miles."

"You think he knows we's follerin' him?" Smoke asked.

"Well, he'll be expecting someone to follow him, and he may guess that I will, but I don't think we're close enough yet for him to have seen us and know for certain how many of us there are or who we are."

They had chosen to camp in a hollow with a creek running through it. After they had picketed their horses on the grass within reach of the creek and made their beds, they eased up to the top of the hollow and took a look around. Off to the north, perhaps ten miles away, they could see the glow of a campfire.

"You don' s'pose he would be sittin' theah drinkin' hot coffee an' keepin' warm while we's lookin' at a long, cold night?" Smoke asked.

"If he built that fire, I'd guess he's waiting in the dark and the cold for someone to be foolish enough to walk into the firelight and get shot."

"You reckon he's likely to leave that fire burnin' an' double back on his trail to try an' sneak up on us?"

"Well, if we were foolish enough to build a fire of our own, or, if there was enough of a moon to give him good light, he might. And we'd best stay alert to that possibility, but I doubt that he's ready to do something like that just yet," Shiloh said. "Why don't you go ahead and try to get some sleep? I'll keep the first watch and wake you when I start to get sleepy."

Both men crawled into their beds to stay warm. Shiloh watched the ridges for any signs of an intruder and listened to the night sounds. As he watched, listened and waited, he prayed silently. Occasionally, he slipped out of his bed and peeked out of the hollow. It was well after midnight when the campfire to the north died out.

"Does that mean he's finally gone to bed?" Shiloh wondered. *"Or has he packed up and moved on? Was that even his fire?"*

When Shiloh began to have trouble staying awake, he nudged Smoke.

"Better let me sleep for a few hours, if you can," he said. "But wake me up if you start to get sleepy."

Smoke looked into the night sky and decided it was about four hours until dawn.

"Ah've had a good sleep. Ah'll try to let you sleep 'til first light."

As Smoke took up the vigil, he, too, prayed silently. At first light, he shook Shiloh, and the two of them broke camp. An hour later, as the sun peeked over the horizon to the east, they stopped, built a fire and made their breakfast. Then they rode on. As they approached the place where they had seen the campfire the night before, they stopped more than a mile away and looked at the trees to the east. Shiloh spent a few minutes looking through his field glasses at the area around the fire ring and into the trees then he handed the glasses to Smoke.

"Have a look," he said. "I think we'd better circle west of those trees and see if we pick up his trail to the north. That ring of rocks where he made the fire, if it was his fire, is well within range of his Whitworth rifle from those trees, and there is no cover for us to approach the trees. If he's gone on, we'll pick up his trail. If he's still in those trees, we'll wait him out."

Smoke handed the field glasses back.

"Ah couldn' see nuthin' of him in the trees, but Ah wouldn' expect to. You reckon he might've rid through them trees an' gone east?"

"That's very possible, and, if we don't find his trail to the north, we'll circle well clear of the trees and have a look to the east."

At the end of a wide half-circle to the west, they picked up the trail again, still heading due north. A few hours later, as the Little Belt Mountains loomed in front of them, the trail veered west of north. They stopped in the middle of the day to rest their horses and to have their noon meal.

"If I'm remembering right," Shiloh said, as they were saddling their horses again. "Caleb told me the Smith River and those mountains come together toward the north end of the range. So Jenkins is either going to have to cross the river to get around, or he's headed to someplace close by."

"They's a ford across the riveh on the trail to Fort Benton," Smoke told him. "If'n Jenkins plans to use it, he'll be turnin' west pretty soon."

Smoke was right. They had ridden another five miles when the tracks turned and led them due west. When they were within sight of the Smith River, they stopped their horses, and Shiloh examined the banks on both sides through the field glasses. Then he scanned the area around the river for possible places for Jenkins to shoot from. When he was done, he again handed the glasses to Smoke.

"Is the water deep enough at the ford that the horses will have to swim?" he asked.

"Prob'ly not this time of year," Smoke told him. "Sometimes in the spring, when the snow's meltin', or after a summer thunderstorm, it gets deep enough an' the current strong enough that folks don' try to cross."

"Looked to me like he went into the water on this side, but I couldn't see any tracks coming out on the other side. Can you tell one way or the other?"

Smoke took another look at the far side of the river.

"Ah cain't tell fo' certain."

"Okay, let's ride south a ways before we head for the ford," Shiloh said. "It looks like he rode straight into the river, but if he turned north once he was in the water, he might have let his horse swim downstream and come back out on this side. If he did, he could be in those bushes on that little rise, and, if we follow his trail straight to the ford, he'll have an easy shot at us long before we reach the water."

Smoke looked carefully at the small rise, trying to see through the bushes or to see any tracks on the ground beyond them. Then he looked further out, trying to find a place where Jenkins might have left his horse.

"If'n he's in them bushes, he left his horse hid someplace, an' Ah don' see no place real close by."

"I didn't either," Shiloh said, as he took the field glasses from

Smoke. "We'll need to ride carefully, and be alert to the possibility that he went south instead of north, but I think if we ride a mile or so south and follow the river north to the ford, we'll be able to tell for certain whether he crossed when we get there. If he didn't cross, we can stay on this side and ride north looking for a place where he might have doubled back. If he is in those bushes and left his horse someplace between that rise and the river, we might be able to get to his horse before he can and set him afoot. Of course, he might have ridden straight across, or he might have gone upstream or down and still come out on the other side, just to slow us down."

"If'n he done that, it's done worked," Smoke said wryly.

"Yep, it has," Shiloh agreed. "But we can't get in a hurry or take any chances chasing this man. He's as good as anyone I've ever seen, better than all but a handful of the soldiers and hunters I've known. For now, he has the advantage."

The two of them turned their horses south and rode away from the rise. When they had covered a mile, they turned west to the river and started back north toward the ford. They looked carefully for any sign that Jenkins had come out of the river on either side and saw none. As they approached the ford, they could see clearly that he had not gone straight across the ford, so they stayed on the east side and continued riding north. Half a mile north of the ford, they found where he had come out of the water and headed east. They stopped again, and Shiloh reached for his field glasses to examine the trail in front of them. Before he could raise the glasses to eye level, they heard the sound of a running horse. Shiloh never saw man or horse, but even without the field glasses, both he and Smoke were able to see the faint trail of dust following the pounding hooves east.

"Okay," Shiloh said. "Now he knows who we are."

"An' he knows at least one of us is good enough not to ride into his ambush."

The two men followed the trail east for an hour, then northeast for the rest of the afternoon. As they had done the previous day, they stopped early to cook their evening meal and moved on to a cold camp for the night. At first light the following morning, they were on the trail again. When the sun came up, they stopped for breakfast.

"If Jenkins is headed for the mountains, he'll be in the trees and set up to ambush us if we follow his trail all the way in," Shiloh said. "I think we should stay on his trail until we're certain that he's headed for the forest, then we need to break off and ride away from his trail and into the trees while we're still out of range of his rifle. Once we're in the trees, too, we can cut back to try to pick up the trail again, but we'll have a better chance of him being within range of our rifles if he takes a shot at one of us."

"How long you reckon it takes him to recharge that muzzle-loader?" Smoke asked.

"Less than a minute," Shiloh said. "If he's real good, maybe a quarter of that."

"So, if'n we ken draw his fire wifout gettin' shot, we'll have at least a count of ten to move closer befo' he ken shoot ag'in wif that rifle."

"Yes, but don't forget that he'll almost certainly have a short gun, and we don't know that the Whitworth is the only rifle he's carrying."

"Well, we'll be in range wif our rifles long befo' a short gun will do him any good," Smoke said. "If'n he's got a repeatin' rifle, we'll be in range wif our rifles by the time he is. An' if'n yo' plan gets us into the trees befo' he gets a shot, we ken get within range if'n we move fast from cover to cover; 'specially, if'n we ken make him miss a couple of times."

"Just remember how good he is," Shiloh said. "And he could have two Whitworths, so don't do anything foolhardy."

"Ah ain't aimin' to."

"Smoke, hunting a man is a little different than hunting an animal. Aside from the fact that he'll be shooting back, this man isn't likely to shoot twice from the same place, so we won't be able to know where his next shot is going to come from. We need to be just as hard to predict. Every time we shoot, we need to move before we shoot again. If we duck down out of sight or move into cover, we need to move under cover and come out in a different place. And we need to try to be random, to keep him from being able to guess our next moves. If you think you know where he is, shoot into the place and left and right of it; that way you might hit him while he's moving. And expect him to try the same thing against you if he does have a repeating rifle."

"Did you learn all that in the war?" Smoke asked.

"Some of it; I learned a lot of it fighting Comanches in Texas."

CHAPTER TWENTY-FIVE

Shiloh and Smoke stopped just short of the crest of a rise to give their horses a blow. They were approaching the foothills of the Little Belt Mountains, and their quarry had still not begun to try to hide his trail. With the field glasses, Shiloh could see the line of Jenkins' trail through the damp grass pointing arrow straight into the trees.

"Okay," Shiloh said. "Now is the time for us to break away from his trail. But he's probably not expecting us to ride straight in on his trail this time, so he likely turned north or south as soon as he reached the trees. You have any angels whispering directions in your ear, Smoke?"

"Nah, suh, Ah don'," Smoke said. "But it's closer to the trees if'n we go north, an' it looks like better ground."

"So you think we should go south?"

"Yes, suh, Ah does."

"Me, too," Shiloh agreed. "We need to move fast and keep moving, and we need to change direction often along the way."

"Ah'll foller you."

Shiloh nudged his bay to the right and spurred him into a gallop, holding him in just a bit. They had to cover more than a mile of open ground, too far for a full-speed sprint. Smoke and

Samson stayed close all the way into the trees. Shiloh did not stop until he was well into the forest, then he pulled his rifle from the scabbard and slid to the ground.

"Let's walk the horses for a while and work our way back toward the place where Jenkins entered the trees," Shiloh said.

The two men led the horses quietly across the soft ground under the huge evergreens, pausing often to look and listen for any movement or sound that might be Jenkins. Both men knew the danger and difficulty of the task before them. They were pursuing a man who would be watching, waiting for them to approach—a man who had the patience to wait and the ability to shoot accurately at long distances. He would be very difficult to see, and he was cunning. Yet neither of them hesitated; they moved purposefully with their rifles at the ready. When they had moved north close to the place where Jenkins' trail entered the trees, Shiloh handed Smoke the reins of his horse.

"Wait here while I take a look," Shiloh said softly.

Shiloh moved silently downhill toward the edge of the trees, and Smoke was wise enough not to let his eyes follow. Instead, he scanned the forest carefully and constantly, not focusing on any one thing but trusting his eyes to pick up movement or anything out of place.

"He turned north as soon as he was in the trees," Shiloh whispered when he returned.

They moved farther up the slope and made their way carefully north. When they had covered half a mile, Shiloh slipped away, down toward the edge of the trees to look again for the tracks of Jenkins' horse; Smoke saw movement in the trees and realized it was Jenkins trying to reposition himself for a shot at Shiloh.

"In the trees on yo' right!" Smoke shouted, as he lifted his rifle and fired at the shadowy figure.

Without pausing, Smoke worked the lever and fired again. Then there was a crashing of tree limbs, and Jenkins was gone. He had scrambled around the trunk of the tree, lowered himself a few feet and dropped fifteen feet to the ground. Then he rolled to his feet and ran directly away from Smoke, picking up his rifle and using the tree trunk as cover. Shiloh fired one round through an opening between the trees, but Jenkins changed direction just as Shiloh fired, and the shot missed.

"Leave the horses!" Shiloh shouted, as he ran after Jenkins.

Smoke tied the two horses to the nearest tree and ran uphill at an angle as he tried to track Jenkins and Shiloh by the few sounds they made running across the soft forest floor. He caught a glimpse of Jenkins moving uphill a hundred yards away and turned at a steeper angle, still running uphill toward a point that would intercept the fleeing man.

Shiloh saw Jenkins turn uphill, and he, too, turned at an angle to shorten the distance. Jenkins disappeared behind a tree less than fifty yards away, and Shiloh ran directly toward it, watching for a rifle barrel to appear from either side of the trunk, looking upward into the tree to see if Jenkins was climbing again. When the entire rifle appeared parallel to the tree trunk and the barrel began tilting toward him, Shiloh dived to the ground and rolled behind the nearest tree on his right. Jenkins never fired; he just turned and ran further up the slope. Shiloh came off the ground and out from behind the tree he had used for cover, moving left in running pursuit. He passed by the tree Jenkins had hidden behind on the left and pressed himself against the next tree he came to. Easing his right eye from behind the tree trunk, he looked for Jenkins. His breathing was a series of gasping rasps, and he held it for a moment, trying to hear any movement that might be Jenkins. He heard the distinct metallic sound of a hammer being cocked and dropped to his knees just as Jenkins fired. Shiloh jumped up and ran to his right in time to see Jenkins running at an angle up the slope to his right, pouring powder into the barrel of the Whitworth as he ran.

"*I've never seen anyone do that before*," Shiloh thought, as Jenkins disappeared over the crest of the rise.

Shiloh immediately turned left and ran straight uphill to cross the rise in a different place. As he reached the crest, he dropped to his knees just short of the branches of a fallen tree and allowed himself to pitch forward into a prone position. Then he crawled upward until his eyes were above the ridge, the top of his head hidden by the trunk of the tree. Looking under the tree trunk, he could see Jenkins thirty yards away, kneeling behind a small tree, replacing the ramrod beneath the barrel of his rifle. As Shiloh eased his Winchester barrel into the gap he was looking through, Jenkins stood and ran to his left. Shiloh followed quickly, but almost immediately he lost sight of Jenkins. Shiloh stopped again and looked out under a thick branch on the left side of a huge tree. Jenkins had vanished. Shiloh waited, looked and listened for a full minute, but there was no sign of Jenkins.

* * * * * * *

As soon as Jenkins had finished reloading the Whitworth rifle, he ran to his left for twenty yards and dropped to the ground. Then he turned ninety degrees to his right and crawled up the slope. When he came to a pair of enormous trees growing less than a foot apart, he crawled behind them and sat up. He pushed the barrel of his rifle into the gap between the tree trunks, cocked the hammer and waited. Jenkins saw Shiloh dart from one tree to another, from his left to his right, and held his fire as he waited to see what Shiloh would do. Shiloh came out from behind the tree to Jenkins' right, took three running steps, turned to Jenkins' left and paused behind another tree.

"*Let's see if he comes out to my right this time,*" Jenkins thought, as he moved the barrel slightly to cover that side of the tree.

Shiloh came out to Jenkins' left and ran almost directly at him before veering behind another tree.

"*Once to the right, once to the left, will he go right again?*"

Jenkins wondered and covered the right side of the tree trunk.

Shiloh came out from behind the tree to Jenkins' left and ran ten yards to another tree.

"Once right, twice left, he'll go right for sure this time," Jenkins thought, and he once again moved the barrel to the right of the tree and prepared to fire.

Shiloh came out from behind the tree in a low crouch, running to Jenkins' right, and Jenkins lowered his point of aim slightly and began to squeeze the trigger. Suddenly the rifle was twisted violently out of his hands, and he was lifted into the air.

"Whut fo' you wants to be shootin' good folks?" Smoke asked, as he slammed Jenkins to the ground hard enough to knock the wind out of him.

Jenkins tried to resist, to twist loose from the crushing grip that squeezed around his neck, but he was powerless against such strength and panicking in breathlessness as the air left his lungs. Smoke dropped a knee into the middle of Jenkins' back, pulled his right arm around and pinned it before turning loose of Jenkins' neck. Then he reached over with his left hand and pulled Jenkins' left arm behind him.

"Ah gots him, Shiloh!" Smoke called. "But Ah needs somethin' to tie him wif."

Shiloh appeared from behind the twin trees and looked down to see Smoke gripping both of Jenkins' wrists in his huge left hand as his right searched for weapons. For a moment Shiloh actually felt sorry for Jenkins, who was still gasping in an effort to get air into his lungs. Then Smoke pulled a Bowie knife from inside Jenkins' left boot, and Shiloh's sympathy disappeared along with his condensing breath in the cold air.

"Where's his rifle?" Shiloh asked. "We can tie him with the sling."

"Ah flung it off thataway." Smoke gestured off to his right.

Shiloh retrieved the rifle and removed the sling. Smoke tied Jenkins securely and lifted him to his feet.

"Ah reckons he needs a minute or two to catch his breath," Smoke said. "Then we ken go get our horses. Ah'm gettin' a little tired of trackin' his horse. If'n he don' remember where it's at, Ah thinks Ah'll just let him walk back to White Sulphur Springs."

"He'll remember," Shiloh said. "Where's your rifle?"

"Leanin' against a tree back yonder," Smoke told him. "Ah wuz gonna shoot him, but it didn' seem like the Good Lord wanted me to. So Ah reckons we'll have to haul him off to jail."

"Jenkins, are you breathing well enough to talk yet?" Shiloh asked.

"Just about," he said. "And I remember exactly where I left my horse."

"All this was about the Northern Pacific railroad laying tracks across the J H Connected, wasn't it?"

Jenkins nodded.

"That railroad project was canceled almost a year before you started shooting people," Shiloh told him. "Now three good men are dead, and you'll likely hang, because of a railroad that was never going to be built."

Jenkins just stared at him in disbelief.

CHAPTER TWENTY-SIX

December, 1876

In the early afternoon on Christmas Eve, Smoke and Cotton drove up to the new ranch house on the J H Connected. In the freight wagon were two large crates and several smaller boxes.

"You folks have a good trip?" Caleb asked, as he walked up to hold the mule team steady, still limping slightly.

"Wuz a mighty good trip," Smoke told him. "It's been a glorious, beautiful day. The snowfall yesterday wuz just enough to give eveh'thin' a fresh, clean look, an' the blue sky an' bright sun today has sho' lifted mah spirits high!"

"How are things coming along at the store, Mr. Storekeeper?" O'Brien asked

"Comin' along right nice," Smoke said. "When we locked Jenkins in the jail, Ah neveh had no idea the gov'ment wuz offerin' a reward fo' catchin' him. Ah still thinks Shiloh should've taken at least half; Ah'd've got mahself shot if'n he hadn' knowed how to avoid gettin' ambushed. An' Jenkins wuz so busy tryin' to shoot Shiloh that he plumb forgot 'bout me. That's how we catched him."

"I would probably have just shot him," O'Brien said.

"Ah wuz goin' to," Smoke admitted. "Had him right in mah sights an' wuz squeezin' the trigger. Ah reckons that's when the Good Lord nudged me a mite. If'n Ah had shot him daid, they wouldn've been no reward, an' Ah might not've been able to buy the sto'."

"Do you suppose I'll ever learn to pay attention when God nudges me?" O'Brien asked.

"Maybe you done has," Smoke said. "You could've shot George Vickers daid, an' you saved him fo' the judge."

"You could be right," O'Brien admitted. "That even surprised me."

The Hadleys and Shiloh walked out onto the porch of the completed section of the new house.

"Good afternoon, Smoke," Sarah said.

"Howdy, ma'am, howdy, Miss Hannah."

"What do you have in the wagon?" Hannah asked excitedly.

"Well, Miss Hannah, we's got yo' Momma's new cookstove an' some other things to go in the new house," Smoke told her. "If'n you bless me wif anotha one of yo' beautiful smiles as a hello greetin', Ah might git excited enough to climb down off'n this wagon an' tote that stuff inside."

Hannah gave him a great big grin.

"Looks heavy enough that even you will need some help," she said. "It's a good thing you brought Cotton with you."

Cotton's ears turned bright red when she flashed another smile directly at him.

"Ah've done worked him half to death today," Smoke told her. "Why don' you drag him off somewheahs an' keep him busy, so's he won' overstrain hisself helpin' me?"

"That'll be fun," Hannah agreed. "We can go for a ride, and I'll show him my meadow. Come on, Cotton, let's go!"

Cotton jumped down from the wagon, and the two of them started for the barn at a run.

"If Swede's still in the barn, he'll want to help saddle the horses," Caleb called after them. "Don't let him; he ain't up to it yet!"

Hannah waved in acknowledgment without turning back.

"Looks like my present to Hannah got here in time," Shiloh said, as he looked at one of the large crates in the wagon. "How much do I owe you with the freight and delivery added in?"

"Well, now, Ah cain't seem to find mah spectacles." Smoke said, as he patted the upper pockets of his overalls.

"I've never knowed you to wear spectacles, Smoke," Caleb said.

"Ah neveh has befo'," Smoke told him. "But Ah must be needin' some, 'cuz Ah cain't see nuthin' but zeroes on Shiloh's bill. Ah reckons that means you don' owe me nuthin' at all, Shiloh."

"You're not going to let me pay you for it, are you?" Shiloh asked.

"Nah, suh, Ah ain't. You rightly should've taken half that reward money, an' Ah couldn' make you take it. Ah'm makin' that crate an' the cost of gettin' it heah a Christmas present to you, an' you cain't make me take no money fo' it. So you just go ahead an' give it away like you wuz plannin' to, an' don' think nuthin' more 'bout no bill."

"Thank you, Smoke, I'll tell Hannah it's a gift from both of us."

"That'll be just fine," Smoke agreed. "Now let's get all uh this stuff inside befo' Cotton runs outta ways to keep Miss Hannah busy."

"If I wuz to be guessin'," Caleb said. "I'd guess she'll be the one keepin' him busy. That girl is plumb full of energy."

"Indeed, she is," O'Brien agreed. "Smoke, why don't we get that cookstove moved into the new kitchen, and I'll start getting it out of the crate?"

"We'd better do that, Smoke," Caleb said. "We shore wouldn't want no Irish lad starvin' to death on Christmas day."

Smoke climbed down from the seat and reached into the wagon for a small-wheeled platform made of heavy boards and stout wheels. When he set it down on the porch, Caleb grinned.

"I can see becomin' a prosperous storekeeper has been an education; that ought to save some carryin' fer you."

"Cotton built it fo' me," Smoke said. "He couldn' remember wheah he got the idea, but it'll sho' ease the strain on mah poor ol' back."

Smoke, Shiloh and O'Brien lifted the crated cookstove out of the wagon and lowered it onto the wheeled platform. Then Smoke and O'Brien rolled the crate into the new kitchen while Caleb held doors open for them.

"Is that what I think it is?" Sarah asked, as she walked over to the wagon and looked at the remaining large crate. When she saw the "Steinway & Sons" label stamped on the crate, she knew she was right. "Where did you find it?"

"When I rode through Cheyenne coming this way a few months back, the freight company owner tried to sell it to me," Shiloh said. "He'd heard I could play and offered it to me for the shipping charges owed. It was taking up a lot of space, and he just wanted to be rid of it. It was ordered by a theater company trying to set up a business in town, but the company had gone bankrupt before it arrived, and no one was there to claim it. It's a parlor grand, brand new in its crate. I didn't have any need for it at the time. When the fire burned Hannah's piano, I sent a letter of inquiry to see if it was still there and offered to buy it for the price I had been quoted."

"Hannah is going to love it," Sarah said.

"I hope so," Shiloh said. "I'll need to get it out of the crate, attach the legs and tune it, so we'll have to keep her out of the front part of the house until morning. I'd like to keep her far enough away that she won't hear me tuning it—that's Cotton's job."

"Hannah and I have already decided that we will wait until

tomorrow to move into the house," Sarah told him. "We shall cook breakfast in the bunkhouse, then the first meal in this new house will be Christmas dinner. We both feel that is a fitting beginning to the blessing God has provided through the wonderful efforts all of you men have made on our behalf."

"Well, you'll have to keep us around for a while longer," Shiloh said. "It will be spring before we can start on the other two rooms."

"It is my hope that all of you will be happy to stay on here well beyond the time required to finish the house," Sarah told him. "Hannah and I will need you for years to come."

"Come spring, you'll need to hire a few more hands," Shiloh told her. "But you won't have any trouble now that Jenkins is locked up."

Sarah was about to say something more when Smoke carried O'Brien bodily out of the house.

"Ah had some trouble convincin' him we needed his help unloadin' this other crate," Smoke explained, as he stood O'Brien on the ground at the back of the wagon. "Did y'all know he's ticklish?"

"They do now," O'Brien said with a mock scowl.

* * * * * * *

Christmas morning dawned bright and beautiful, and breakfast was a fun and festive occasion. But Hannah was especially anxious to get it over with; she knew there were presents waiting in the new house—she was hoping her mother had remembered the porcelain doll she had seen in the store—but, mostly, she was looking forward to moving into her new room, and she was excited at the prospect of Christmas dinner. The Reardons were coming, and Dr. Carson and his wife had been invited along with several other families from the church. Smoke and Cotton had stayed the night. Hannah was truly looking forward to the festivities and fellowship.

"Smoke, how's that new man you hired workin' out on the farm?" Caleb asked, as they were gettin' up from the table.

"Jacob's doin' a real fine job," Smoke said. "Ah told him it wuz just temporary 'til mah folks move out heah in the spring, but he's a hard worker an' needs to make a livin' fo' his family, so Ah'm hopin' Ah ken find someone to take him on permanent by then. He says he's a blacksmith by trade, an' a good one, so Ah thought Ah'd talk to Benson at the livery stable an' see if maybe he could set up a smithy theah—it'd be good fo' the both of 'em an' good fo' the town. Jacob's sho' doin' good work on that cookstove you give me, Miz Hadley; we's still waitin' on a few trim pieces, but it's lookin' real nice—sho' better than if Ah'd done all the work mahself. Jenny's goin' to be real pleased."

"I hope so," Sarah told him. "We are all looking forward to meeting her; you have told us so much about her, I feel as though I know her already." She looked around and noticed Hannah clearing away the breakfast dishes. "Hannah, you may leave those for now. I think everyone is ready to go on up to the new house. You and I need to start the turkey Mr. Olsen brought in; it will need to cook for several hours. Then we can all open presents. I can take care of those dishes by myself today. You just enjoy the day and the company."

"Do you need anything carried up to your new kitchen?" O'Brien asked.

"Yes, thank you, Mr. O'Brien, I have some things boxed up that I will need to start the turkey. Eventually, everything in this temporary kitchen will need to be moved."

O'Brien gathered up the box Sarah had indicated.

"I'll just be taking this now," he said. "And I'll come back for anything else you need for today's dinner."

"Caleb," Shiloh said. "I think you can put Michael Darlin' in charge of moving Mrs. Hadley's kitchen; he seems to have volunteered for that duty. So I guess you and I will need to move the things in their rooms down here to their new rooms in the house."

"We can move 'em in the wagon after dinner," Caleb said.

* * * * * * *

Caleb started a fire in the new cookstove while Sarah and Hannah prepared the turkey for baking; once the bird was in the oven, the three of them joined the others in the front room. Shiloh had positioned himself and the other men in a row in front of the new piano, so Hannah did not see it as she walked into the room. Hannah went directly to the Christmas tree and picked up a package.

"Mother, shall I give these out now?"

"Please do."

Everyone had a gift to open; some were practical items of clothing or tools. Cotton received several books. Among other gifts, Hannah discovered that Sarah had remembered the porcelain doll.

"Oh, Mother, thank you!" Hannah exclaimed.

Sarah returned Hannah's hug and kiss then whispered in her ear.

"I believe you have one more gift from Shiloh and Smoke."

Hannah whirled around and looked beneath the tree, but she saw no overlooked gift. When she turned back with questioning eyes, the men had moved, and she saw the piano for the first time. With a gleeful shriek, she ran to the piano and sat down on the stool. She rubbed the beautiful black finish of the wood with her fingertips before gently opening the cover to expose the keys. She raised her hands to the keyboard and rested her fingertips on the keys. Then she stood up and walked over to Shiloh and Smoke. She wrapped an arm around each of them, and with tears streaming down her cheeks she looked up at them.

"Thank you so much," she told them. "You can't know how

much this means to me."

"We love you, Hannah, all of us," Shiloh told her. "And we wanted you to know how much you mean to us."

"What shall I play for you?" she asked.

"Whatever you wish."

"Cotton, my music burned in the fire, but I think I can play 'O Holy Night' from memory," Hannah said. "It would be a perfect song for this day. Would you sing the lyrics while I play?"

Cotton was obviously embarrassed to be asked, but he quietly nodded and moved to stand near her as she returned to the piano. Nearly everyone present had heard Hannah play, but most had not heard Cotton sing. He was a gangly teenager, a boy just becoming a man, but he had a beautiful baritone voice, and he loved to sing as much as Hannah loved to play the piano. Sarah cried unashamedly at the beauty of the performance and for the gift of God's love revealed in the words of the Christmas hymn. The men were equally moved and fought back tears deemed unmanly in their society. Even Lars Olsen, who had yet to meet the Lord Jesus on his personal road to Damascus, was mesmerized by the song and the two young Christian performers.

* * * * * * *

Christmas morning passed in music and conversation. Hannah continued to play, and she insisted that Shiloh play as well. Both picked music appropriate to the day with lyrics known to Cotton. As the guests arrived, more conversation was followed by more musical requests. Soon, the front room of the new log house was filled with laughter and song, as Cotton encouraged everyone to join him in singing the words most knew by heart. The music and conversation spilled over into the kitchen, as the arriving women joined Sarah in preparing dinner, bringing favorite dishes and desserts with them as they came.

Before announcing dinner, Sarah stood in the doorway between her new kitchen and parlor and enjoyed the sounds of joy resounding from the walls of her home. Caleb was sitting on the stone hearth; he had taken responsibility for keeping the fire ablaze. Cotton and Shiloh were at the piano. The rooms were filled with friends and with loyal men she had come to regard as family. But she felt a sudden and deep sadness as she realized that Jonathan would never again share such moments with her. Hannah leaned against her and looked into her eyes as if she was able to read her thoughts.

"I miss Father so much," Hannah said. "I know you must, too. But I hope Shiloh doesn't leave us now that he thinks he's almost completed the mission God sent him here to accomplish. He is so good, and I love him so much. Smoke told me that the piano was really Shiloh's gift to me, that his part was more in payment of a debt to Shiloh. Is it wrong for me to love Shiloh so much?"

"No, honey, it is not wrong, and I love him, too," Sarah told her. "But Shiloh must go where God leads him, and we must be willing to let God use him according to His purpose."

Sarah held Hannah close and straightened up to announce Christmas dinner.

"Reverend Pearson, would you offer our thanks to God for this new home, for the fellowship of friends and brothers and sisters in Christ and for the blessings of a bounteous feast in celebration of the birth of His Son and our Savior."

"I'd be happy to, Mrs. Hadley," the pastor told her. "But I believe you just did."

Sarah laughed.

"I suppose I did, but I am quite certain God has given you something special to say today, and I very much want to hear your words."

"Very well," he said. "Please bow your heads."

* * * * * * *

As the afternoon passed swiftly and the guests had to leave, including Smoke and Cotton, the men of the J H Connected finished moving the Hadleys from the bunkhouse into their new home. When the moving was done, Sarah invited the men to remain in the parlor until suppertime.

"We'll have leftovers, of course," she said. "Not even Michael Darlin' could have finished off the meal brought today by our friends. If any of you are interested, I have some wine and brandy saved from the fire. And Mr. O'Brien, I have 'a bit o' the Irish' for you." She handed him a small bottle of Irish whiskey.

O'Brien accepted it with a warm smile.

"Thank you, Mrs. Hadley, this is much appreciated."

"So are all of you," she said. "Merry Christmas."

Michael O'Brien offered to share his prize with the others, but Lars Olsen drank a glass of wine, and Caleb chose brandy. Shiloh asked for coffee, and Hannah went back to her new piano to play the Chopin nocturne she loved so much.

"I think the coffee is gone, Shiloh," Sarah told him. "I shall make a fresh pot just for you. Would you like to wait for it in the kitchen?"

"Yes, thank you."

Shiloh followed Sarah into the kitchen and sat down at the table; he watched in silence as she went about the ordinary task of brewing coffee. But the silence was uncomfortable for him. When the coffee pot was on the stove, Sarah sat down across the table from him, but she did not break the silence.

"Sarah, do you remember that I told you as a young man I was terrified of talking to young ladies?" Shiloh asked.

Sarah only nodded, looking directly into his eyes.

"I think I have become that young man again," he said. "I need to tell you something, but I am very much afraid that you will be offended."

"You have nothing to fear from me, Shiloh," she told him. "And I can think of nothing you would say that could offend me."

"Sarah Hadley, I love you, and I want very much to marry you, but I can't think of any reason why you would want to marry me."

"I would want to marry you, because I love you, Shiloh."

"Would you give me the great joy and do me the honor of becoming Mrs. Paul Daniel Clifton?"

"It would give me great joy to do so."

Sarah laughed, and Shiloh breathed.

"Shall we tell Hannah?" she asked. "She loves you as much as I do."

As they both stood up, they turned to see Hannah standing in the doorway in front of Caleb, O'Brien and Swede; Hannah was giggling.

"I already know," she said and ran to join them.

THE END

ABOUT THE AUTHOR

A native Texan, a military veteran and once upon a time a cowboy, Robert Starr now lives, works and writes in eastern Washington. Starr is an avid outdoorsman and loves to hike and camp with his wife, Alyssa, their three grown children and four grandchildren.

As a finalist in the 2012 Deep River Books writing contest, **Until Shiloh Comes** was awarded a *Certificate of Merit*. In the 2013 contest, Starr received a second *Certificate of Merit* for his novel, **A Walk in the Wilderness**.

Made in the USA
San Bernardino, CA
30 July 2016